CRUSHES, BLUSHES, AND FRIENDS FOREVER

best friends Club, ink™
Stick Together. Friends Forever!™

First published by Parragon in 2009

Parragon
Queen Street House
4 Queen Street
Bath BA1 1HE, UK

For other great BFC INK™ products check out our website at www.bfcink.com

ISBN 978-1-4075-7858-3

Printed in U.S.A.

Please retain information for future reference.

Written by Becky Brookes, Rennie Brown, Sarah Delmege,
Kirsty Neale and Caroline Plaisted

CRUSHES, BLUSHES, AND FRIENDS FOREVER

Parragon

Bath • New York • Singapore • Hong Kong • Cologne • Delhi • Melbourne

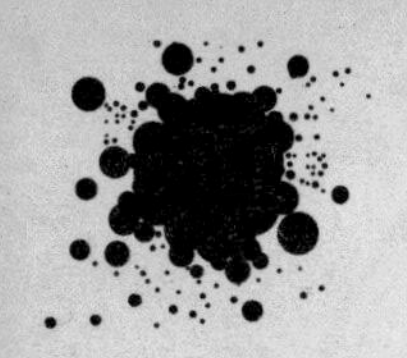

CONTENTS:

My Diary
by Calista
2-1=

Friday, 8:05 am—MY BIRTHDAY!!

Yay! It's my birthday! I am officially a year older and loads wiser.

Stuff I know now that I didn't know one year ago:

1. That my friends are really GREAT and I can count on them always. Since we started the BFC—Best Friends' Club—we've had some amazing fun.
2. What it's like to live in Canada. We moved there because of Dad's job last year, then came back. I missed my friends soooooooo much!
3. That Gianna Harris is ok. She hangs out with BFC's sworn enemy, Dina the Diva, but I found out this year she isn't as bad as Dina.
4. That Kaitlin rocks. She's the newest member of the BFC and I didn't know her a year ago. She's a great designer.

There's probably loads more stuff, but for now, I'm too excited about going to school and seeing my friends to remember it all. And, hey—it's my BIRTHDAY!

Friday, 12:55 pm

What is going on? No one's even mentioned my birthday. Not one teeny-weeny, handmade-by-Kaitlin card. Not even Aliesha doing her usual star-of-the-show thing and standing on a desk singing "Happy Birthday". Right now, I'm in the girls' bathroom, by myself, writing this, when I should be outside, trying to persuade my friends not to embarrass me by singing. This must be the worst birthday in the history of the world.

Friday 5:15 pm

I sooo have the best friends! Like they'd forget my birthday. The whole thing was a total scam and I fell for it. DUH! OK, so I got home in a totally foul mood, thinking everyone had forgotten me. But then, when I walked through the front door—major surprise!

It turned out Addison, Kaitlin, Noelle, and Aliesha had checked with Mom and Dad, who agreed they could throw me this totally amazing birthday party. They'd invited Gianna, plus Addison's brothers, Jake and Josh, and Jake's friends, Elliot and Ben (who is now officially Noelle's boyfriend). Addison, who's the club organizer, had taken

care of snacks and drinks, Noelle sent the invitations, Kaitlin did decorations, and Aliesha chose the music. The only thing that wasn't completely awesome was the fact that they were all wearing party stuff and I was in my school clothes.

"Upstairs!" said Aliesha, sounding like my mom. Which is where I am now, changing into the amazing new top the BFCs chipped in to buy me as a present.

Saturday, 10:20 am

Stuff that was great about my party:

1. Making up dance routines to Aliesha's new Beat Boyz CD.
2. The food—mini-pizzas, nachos, and chocolate ice cream. Yum!
3. Playing party games, especially when we made it girls vs boys, and the girls won.
4. My heart-shaped birthday cake, with "Friends rock!" written on top in icing.

Stuff that wasn't great about my party:

1. Dad getting home from work and deciding he "wanted to boogie." Major embarrassment!
2. Gianna hanging around Jake, flirting with him, dancing with him, and generally looking like she was getting a massive crush on him.
3. Jake—who has been Kaitlin's crush for ages—flirting back and looking as if he likes Gianna, too.

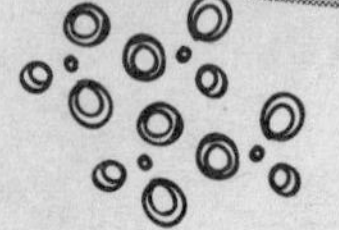

EEK!

I seriously hope it was just what Aliesha calls "party fever." If Gianna and Jake really like each other, Kaitlin will be devastated.

Official BFC Dictionary

Party fever (n): When you're having so much dancing, cake-eating, and general party fun, even a total geek can seem cool. Fever (and coolness of geek) unlikely to last after the party ends.

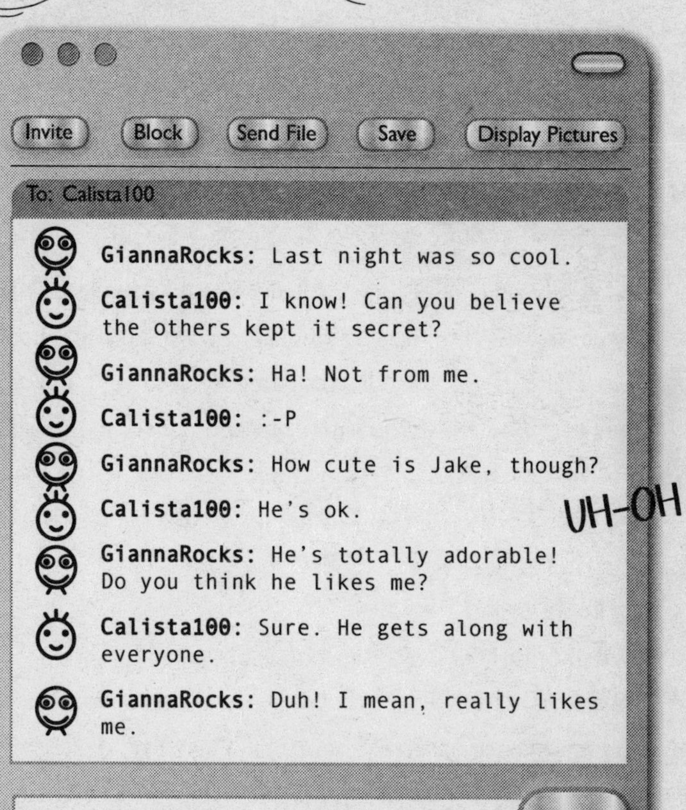
Invite
Block
Send File
Save
Display Pictures
To: Calista100
GiannaRocks: Last night was so cool.
Calista100: I know! Can you believe the others kept it secret?
GiannaRocks: Ha! Not from me.
Calista100: :-P
GiannaRocks: How cute is Jake, though?
Calista100: He's ok.
UH-OH
GiannaRocks: He's totally adorable! Do you think he likes me?
Calista100: Sure. He gets along with everyone.
GiannaRocks: Duh! I mean, really likes me.
Calista100: Gotta go—Mom's calling me.
Send

1+1=

I know—total cop-out, but what was I supposed to say? I think Jake likes her, which would be fantastic if only Kaitlin didn't have a crush on him, too. And because it happened at my party, it feels like the whole thing is my fault.

Monday, 4:15 pm

Today was a total disaster. All morning at school, Kaitlin was really down in the dumps. We all tried not to talk about Jake or the party, in case it upset her even more, but then, at lunchtime, Aliesha—who isn't exactly a genius at keeping quiet—couldn't hold it in any longer.

"Are you ok?" she said to Kaitlin, as we ate our sandwiches in the cafeteria.

Kaitlin shrugged.

"It's Jake, isn't it?" said Aliesha Blabbermouth.

Kaitlin looked up with this awful expression on her face.

"He likes Gianna," she said hoarsely. "I know he does. It was so obvious at the party. I know we're not going out or anything," she said, "but I thought maybe there might be a chance he liked me." She bit her lip, and I knew she was trying not to cry. "Gianna likes him back, doesn't she?" said Kaitlin, looking straight at me.

Kaitlin & Jake ???

I panicked. "I don't know. She didn't . . . I think so, yes."

"How could you?" said a voice behind me.

I spun round and saw, to my total horror, that Gianna was sitting at the next table.

"I don't want everyone knowing I like Jake," she said furiously.

"I didn't mean to tell everyone," I said, "but Kaitlin likes him too, and . . ."

"Shut up!" yelled Kaitlin, and stormed off.

"I'm really sorry," I told Gianna.

"Forget it," she snapped. "You obviously can't keep your mouth shut about anything."

Honestly, if there was a prize for saying the wrong thing at the wrong time, I'd be a world champion.

Monday, 7:30 pm

I've just had an idea. Maybe if we know who Jake really likes, we can straighten everything out. How do we find out what Jake's thinking? Well, duh—I'm best friends with his sister!

Action replay of the phone convo between me and Addison:
I said:
I have this idea about how to settle things between Kaitlin and Gianna. I need your help.
Then Addison said:
No problemo. What can I do?
Stand by for brilliant plan:
Talk to Jake and find out who he likes.
Addison, sounding firm:
Uh-uh. No way.
Uh, hello?
Don't you care how upset Kaitlin is?
So, Addison said:
Of course I do, but I don't want to stick my nose in between her and Jake.
Me, getting seriously ticked off:
Is that what you think I'm doing, sticking my nose in?
Brrrrrr....
Addison hung up on me!

Tuesday, 12:35 pm

Addison isn't talking to me. Neither are Kaitlin and Gianna. Kaitlin is talking to Addison, but not to Gianna. Addison isn't talking to Gianna either.

"Not you too," said Aliesha, plonking down next to me at lunchtime. I was sitting by myself, pulling pieces of lettuce out of my sandwich. "Seriously, being miserable is like some kind of contagious disease around here today."

"Don't be mean," said Noelle. I smiled at her gratefully.

"I feel like this whole mess is my fault," I explained to them. "All I wanted was to stop Kaitlin and Gianna from getting hurt, and now I've dragged Addison into it too."

"It's not that bad," said Aliesha.

"It is," I argued. "BFC members aren't supposed to let boys come between us, but we totally have."

"There's only one thing to do," said Aliesha. Me and Noelle looked at her. "Duh!" said Aliesha. "Emergency meeting."

Tuesday, 4:10 pm

Aliesha and Noelle are the best friends ever. The minute school was over, they dragged me back to their house so we could hatch a plan. This is what we came up with...

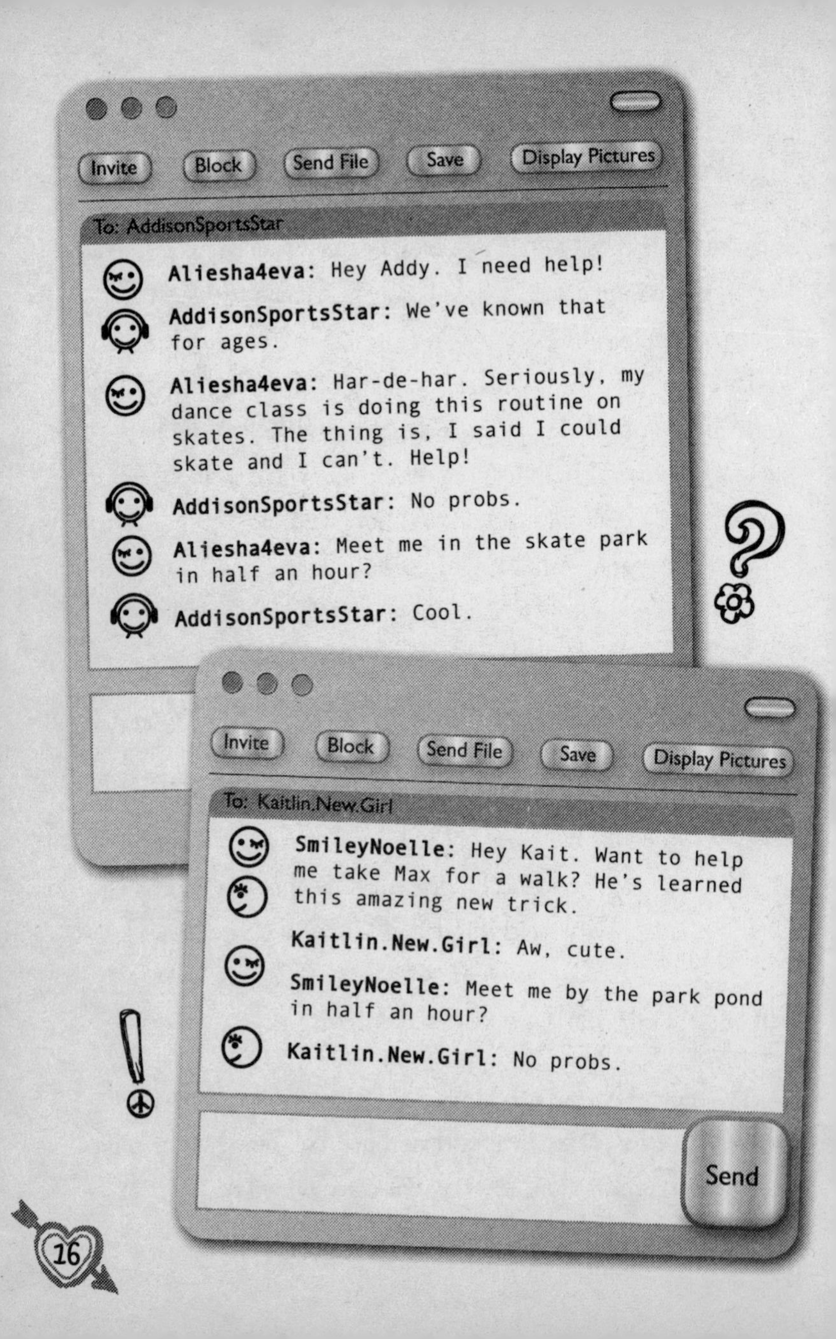
Invite
Block
Send File
Save
Display Pictures
To: AddisonSportsStar
Aliesha4eva: Hey Addy. I need help!
AddisonSportsStar: We've known that for ages.
Aliesha4eva: Har-de-har. Seriously, my dance class is doing this routine on skates. The thing is, I said I could skate and I can't. Help!
AddisonSportsStar: No probs.
Aliesha4eva: Meet me in the skate park in half an hour?
AddisonSportsStar: Cool.
Invite
Block
Send File
Save
Display Pictures
To: Kaitlin.New.Girl
SmileyNoelle: Hey Kait. Want to help me take Max for a walk? He's learned this amazing new trick.
Kaitlin.New.Girl: Aw, cute.
SmileyNoelle: Meet me by the park pond in half an hour?
Kaitlin.New.Girl: No probs.
Send

"Cool," said Aliesha as Noelle logged out. "Two down, one to go. You know what you're doing?" she asked me.

I nodded, and pulled on my jacket.

Operation FBB—mission plan:

Stage 1: Calista goes to Gianna's house to apologize.

Stage 2: Aliesha meets Addison in the skate park.

Stage 3: Noelle meets Kaitlin by the pond in the park.

Stage 4: Calista goes home to pick up mission supplies, then back to Noelle and Aliesha's.

Stage 5: Aliesha falls and pretends to twist her ankle so Addison has to help her walk home.

Stage 6: Noelle secretly throws a dog-biscuit in the pond, so Max jumps in after it.

Stage 7: Noelle persuades Kaitlin to come home with her and clean pond slime off Max.

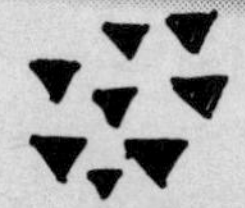

Tuesday, 8:30 pm

We did it—YAY!

Noelle and Kaitlin got back to the Roberts' house with Max just as Addison and Aliesha limped through the door.

There was an awkward silence, then me and Addison both said "I'm really sorry," at exactly the same time.

"I shouldn't have jumped down your throat," I said. "I only wanted to keep Kaitlin from getting hurt."

"I know," Addison nodded. "I feel awful that it's my brother who's causing so much trouble."

"It's not his fault I've got a crush on him," said Kaitlin.

I bit my lip nervously. "I've talked to Gianna. She said she'd totally forgotten you had a crush on him and she's really sorry for flirting with him at the party. She's not going to do anything about the fact she likes him. She said friends are more important than boys."

"Totally," nodded Addison.

"Definitely," I said, "and I know the perfect way to celebrate." I reached into my bag and took out a box.

"Leftover birthday cake!" I said, pulling the lid off.

"Friends ro?" smiled Kaitlin, reading what was left of the icing on top.

"Yup," I giggled. "They sooo do!"

My Diary
by Kaitlin

sunday 10 am

Three reasons why Gianna Harris is RUINING my life!

1. She is best buddies with Dina Hart (the 'Diva' has tried to break up the BFC on numerous occasions, 'nuff said).
2. Her friend, Calista, is my friend too. Which makes it totally awkward for EVERYONE, considering . . .
3. Gianna has developed an almighty mega-crush on my crush, Jake!!!

Which would be fine if she was mean, like Dina. But she's not. And what's worse, Addison's older brother seems to like her too.

I mean, I've had a crush on Jake for AGES and I even thought he felt the same way. When Dad married his girlfriend, Jen (who also happens to be mom to my baby bro, Billy), he let me invite my BFC buddies,

Jake, and Jake's friend, Ben.

Me and Jake had a super swoon-y dance together, but nothing's really happened since then. So I was TOTALLY looking forward to Calista's surprise b'day party.

But Miss Perfect Gianna had to turn up and change EVERYTHING. I can't compete with someone like that. No way!!!

Three reasons why I am NOT Gianna Harris:

1. I'm not a born flirt.
2. I'm not a huge fan of sports.
3. I'm Kaitlin Queen Klutz (I've lost count of how many blushtastic moments I've had since I started at Green Meadow Middle School).

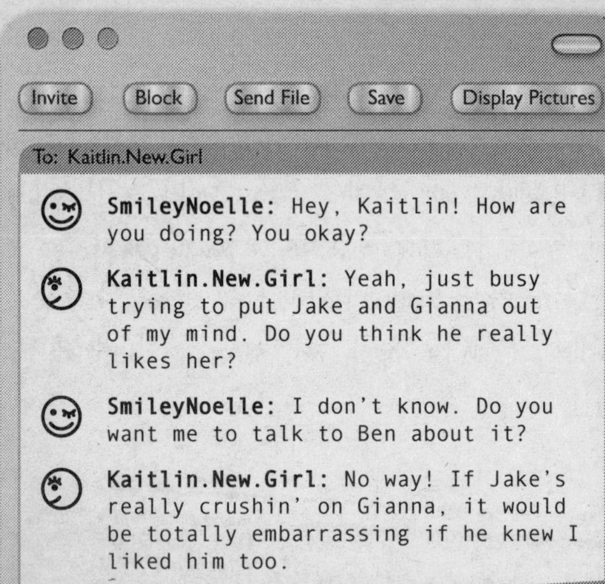
Invite
Block
Send File
Save
Display Pictures
To: Kaitlin.New.Girl
SmileyNoelle: Hey, Kaitlin! How are you doing? You okay?
Kaitlin.New.Girl: Yeah, just busy trying to put Jake and Gianna out of my mind. Do you think he really likes her?
SmileyNoelle: I don't know. Do you want me to talk to Ben about it?
Kaitlin.New.Girl: No way! If Jake's really crushin' on Gianna, it would be totally embarrassing if he knew I liked him too.

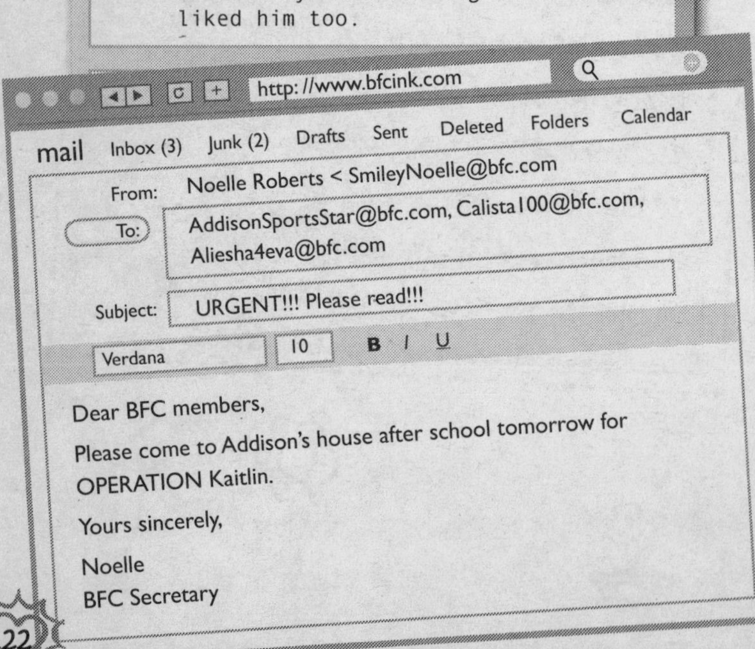
http://www.bfcink.com
mail
Inbox (3)
Junk (2)
Drafts
Sent
Deleted
Folders
Calendar
From: Noelle Roberts < SmileyNoelle@bfc.com
To: AddisonSportsStar@bfc.com, Calista100@bfc.com, Aliesha4eva@bfc.com
Subject: URGENT!!! Please read!!!
Verdana
10
B I U
Dear BFC members,
Please come to Addison's house after school tomorrow for OPERATION Kaitlin.
Yours sincerely,
Noelle
BFC Secretary

OPERATION Kaitlin? Nothing the BFC can possibly do will make me feel better. I just have to find a new crush. Simple!

monday 7:30 pm

There we all were, in Addison's living room, listening to Aliesha as she chaired the meeting.

"Ahem," she began. "We are gathered here today cos we all know there's this problem with Kaitlin and Gianna..."

Just then, in strolled Ben and Jake, stuffing their faces with chips. Jake had obviously caught the end of Aliesha's sentence, cos he spluttered: "Gianna? Is she here?" Even when he's asking for some other girl and spraying potato chips out of his mouth, he's still cute. I've got it bad!

"Uh no," Noelle grinned, jumping up to give Ben a hug. "We were just talking about our favorite TV hunks."

"Do you know who Gianna likes?" Jake continued. Oh, puh-lease! The boy was obsessed. So I left the room to take a few deep breaths and compose myself in the Jacksons' bathroom (classy, huh?).

After about five minutes, I headed back toward the living room. But what I heard next made me stop in my tracks...

Action replay of a conversation between Jake, Ben, and the BFC:

They must have been talking about me, cos I heard Jake say:

What, me and Kaitlin? Nah, not really.

Then Aliesha replied:

But, why not? I thought you liked her?

Then Addison said:

Ugh, this conversation is seriously creepy. I'm outta here!

And Jake paused before adding quietly:

I just don't think Kaitlin's into me in THAT way. Besides, she's really shy, so it's kind of hard to talk to her.

Just then, the door swung open, and I was standing face to face with Addison. Jake looked up at me and stopped talking. I blushed, he blushed, Addison blushed. It was Blush Central.

"Is anyone hungry? I'm starving!" said Noelle, leaping to my rescue. "I spied some nachos on the kitchen counter earlier. Come on, Kaitlin . . ."

A few minutes later, we brought a couple of bowls of snacks into the sitting room. Jake and Ben had already made a hasty exit.

"Well," said Noelle, smiling brightly, "at least Jake didn't say he DIDN'T like you, Kait."

I made a face. "But he didn't say he liked me either," I sniffed.

Aliesha put her arm around my shoulders. "Time to put our plan into action," she said.

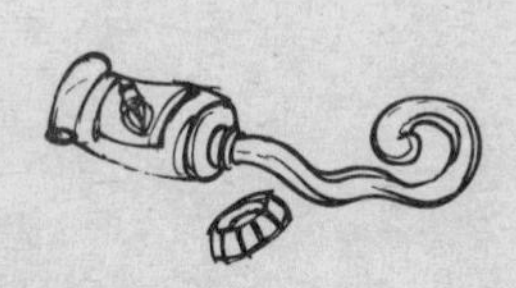

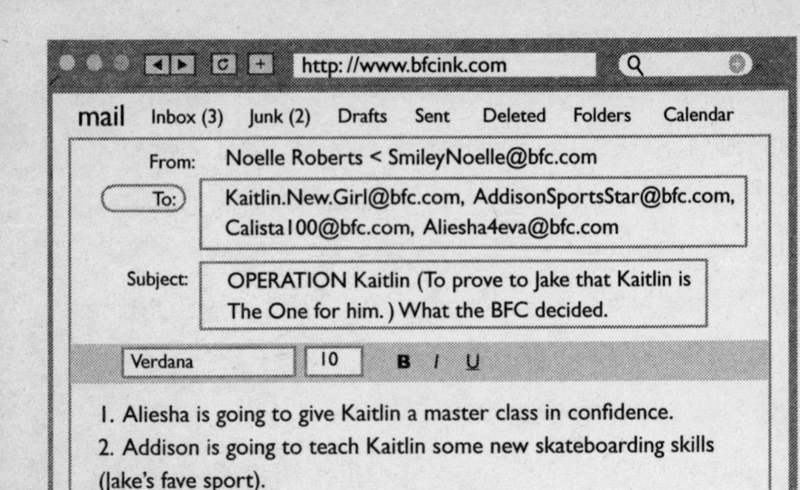

http: //www.bfcink.com

mail Inbox (3) Junk (2) Drafts Sent Deleted Folders Calendar

From: Noelle Roberts < SmileyNoelle@bfc.com

To: Kaitlin.New.Girl@bfc.com, AddisonSportsStar@bfc.com, Calista100@bfc.com, Aliesha4eva@bfc.com

Subject: OPERATION Kaitlin (To prove to Jake that Kaitlin is The One for him.) What the BFC decided.

Verdana 10 B I U

1. Aliesha is going to give Kaitlin a master class in confidence.
2. Addison is going to teach Kaitlin some new skateboarding skills (Jake's fave sport).
3. I'm going to give her some tips on flirting.
4. Calista is going to try and cool Gianna off about Jake. Apparently, this jock in our class, Dougie, really likes her (which is good because Gianna used to like him before she met Jake)!!!

monday 7 pm

Aliesha's just left after talking me through her top mega-confidence boosters:

My (Tried And Tested) Mega-confidence Boosters (by Aliesha)

1. Learn to love yourself.
2. Remember that no one is better or worse than you.
3. Don't take yourself too seriously.
4. Be true to yourself.
5. If all else fails, think of someone super-confident and pretend you're them instead.

"Aren't points four and five kind of saying opposite things?" I asked Aliesha.

"Look, do you want Jake to like you or not?" she asked. I nodded my head. "Well then, you have to do whatever it takes to get him to fall for you."

wednesday 7:35 pm

How am I going to remember everything Addison just showed me at the skate park??? She tried to show me some cool tricks to impress Jake, but I've spent most of this evening ON MY BUTT. I just can't help thinking that this isn't me.

friday 6 pm

Aw, good old Noelle. She didn't totally feel comfortable when Aliesha asked her to give me some flirting tips.

"I have NO idea how to attract boys," she told me yesterday evening. "So I brought along Aliesha's latest copy of 'The Juice'—there's bound to be some tips in

here." We both had a giggle at the "Dishing The Dirt On Being A Flirt" article (written by my very own journalist sister, Katie).

Dishing the dirt on being a flirt

Try our top tips on getting the man of your dreams.

1. Flutter your eyelashes. This will draw his attention to your pretty peepers.
2. Flick your hair from side to side, and twist a few delicate strands in your fingers. Your guy will be wowed by your glossy locks.
3. Touch his arm from time to time. This will make him feel as if he's the most important person on the planet.
4. Laugh at his jokes. He'll think you have a similar sense of humor.
5. And when you're not laughing, smile. He'll think you're friendly, fun, and pretty.

BY KATIE MCCARTHY

My sister wrote this!?

Seriously, have I just been transported back in time to the 1940s??? Aren't women of today encouraged NOT to do the very things my sister is writing about??? Still, if it means winning Jake's heart, it's worth a try...

So now I have tomorrow evening to find my confidence, become an overnight skateboarding sensation and prime my flirting techniques. No problemo (I wish).

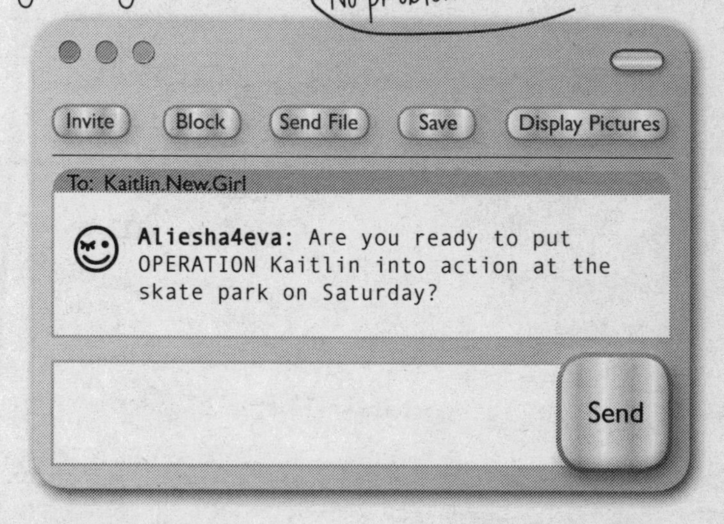

saturday 4 pm

I've just gotten back from the skate park after EMBARRASSING MYSELF TO THE MAX in front of Jake.

Dishing the Dirt on Being a Loser

By Kaitlin McCarthy

FOREVER!

Try my top tips on scaring the man of your dreams.

1. Flutter your eyelashes, causing the man of your dreams to look at you weirdly and say, "Is there something wrong with your eyes?".
2. Flick your hair from side to side, and head-butt the man of your dreams, giving him a headache.
3. Laugh at his jokes. OR, in my case, all the time (I was so nervous, I couldn't figure out what was/wasn't a joke, so I just laughed at everything).
4. Then, when your confidence has reached ZERO, pretend you're someone else (since Aliesha is the most confident person I know, I picked her), and burst into the latest Beat Boyz song (well, it is a very Aliesha-ish thing to do). If he isn't already thinking you should be carted off to the loony bin, this should seal the deal.
5. And finally, fall on your butt before you even attempt to do a skateboarding trick.

Why did I take the advice on flirting from my sister's article? She doesn't even HAVE a boyfriend. What was I thinking?!

saturday 5 pm

I am still in pain. I hadn't even put one foot on Addison's board when I tripped on my way to the ramp on the only patch of uneven ground ahead of me. I landed on the front tip of the board, hurting my already bruised butt, and causing the board to flip up into the air and settle a few feet away from Jake.

Way to go, Kaitlin. Jake is pining for you now. NOT!

saturday 7 pm

Guess who just dropped in??? JAKE!!! Apparently, Addison explained to him why I was acting so weird (she didn't mention that I liked him or anything—just that I was trying out some tips from a magazine article). And get this . . . he wants to go for a walk! With me!! Tomorrow!!! I'm gonna call Noelle to see if I can borrow

her crazy Jack Russell, Max. He's so dippy, he's bound to outdo me on the klutz front. Well, that's the plan anyway.

sunday 5:30 pm

Max is OUT OF CONTROL. He only dragged me through a slippery pile of mud—it's the second time in the space of two days that Jake has seen me fall flat!!!

Luckily, he found the whole thing funny. Then, when Jake tried to pull me up, he slipped, and before I knew it, we were both sitting on the ground, splattered in mud. After that, I kind of loosened up a bit and we had a really good time. I think we have the same kooky sense of humor.

And guess what else? Jake thinks I'm cute AND funny. And that's without a Beat Boyz song, skateboarding trick, or a fluttering eyelash in sight.

Okay, so we may not be an item (yet) but at least he likes me just the way I am, and that's cool by me.

PS: I just got this text from Calista:

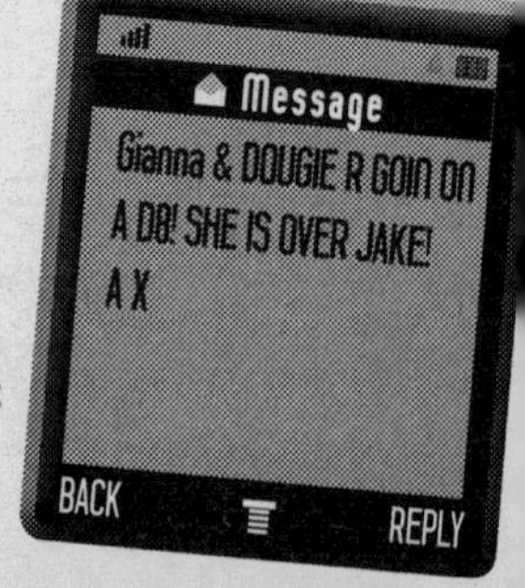

My diary
by Noelle

Saturday 4:23 pm

Aliesha is in a bad mood. A really BAD, door-slamming mood.

The thing is, usually when Aliesha is in a bad mood, she sounds off to me and the rest of the Best Friends' Club. But this time she won't tell anyone what's upsetting her. It's totally out of character.

"She'll tell you when she's ready," Kaitlin whispered during today's BFC meeting. "Don't worry about her so much, Noelle."

But I can't help it. I mean, she's my identical twin sister. I was born to worry about her.

Saturday 6:32 pm

http: //www.bfcink.com

mail Inbox (3) Junk (2) Drafts Sent Deleted Folders Calendar

From: Noelle Roberts < SmileyNoelle@bfc.com

To: KaitlinNewGirl@bfc.com, AddisonSportsStar@bfc.com, Calista100@bfc.com, Aliesha4eva@bfc.com

Subject: BFC minutes (i.e. stuff we said and did)

Verdana 10 B I U

Hiya Clubbers!

Here are the official minutes of today's Best Friends' Club meeting . . .

Place of meeting: Saturday morning, Addison's bedroom.

Members present:

Club member: Noelle—Position in club: Secretary

Club member: Kaitlin—Position in club: Designer

Club member: Aliesha—Position in club: Chairperson

Club member: Addison—Position in club: Events organizer

Club member: Calista—Position in club: Treasurer

Discussion: New computerized calendar

Conclusion: Everyone liked the idea of having a BFC computer diary—which is a good thing because I spent all last week setting it up!

Action: Just a few more tweaks and the BFC online calendar should be up and running. Yay! It will be soo cool—just you wait!

Yours sincerely,

Noelle

BFC Secretary

Saturday 8:34 pm

I don't believe it! Ben just stood me up! I just went over to his house with loads of snacks to eat in front of the DVD and his mom said that he'd gone to Jake's.

We definitely had a date tonight. How could he forget?

When I told Aliesha about it she just shrugged and said, "Oh well, maybe he's just not that into you."

Sympathetic? NOT!

Sunday 2:45 pm

I spoke to Ben on the phone this morning and he swears that I told him I couldn't come over to watch DVDs because I was busy with a BFC thing. Huh?

I soooo don't remember canceling our date. What's he talking about?

Monday 5:54 pm

Aliesha's still in a mood. I tried asking her what's wrong at lunch and she just said:

If you have to ask, there's no point in telling you!

Kaitlin was just coming around the corner at the time, so she overheard everything. Hang on, she just IM-ed me.

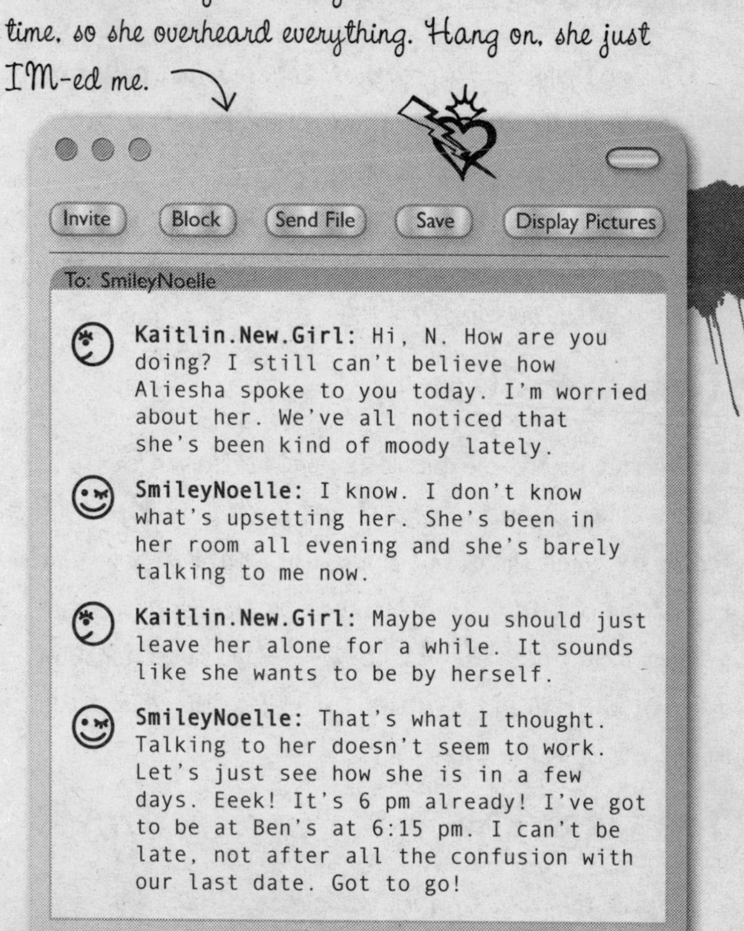

Monday 8 pm

OK, so I officially feel bad. Aliesha just asked if I wanted to go for a burger after school tomorrow but I had to tell her I was meeting Ben.

Then she said, "Well, if my twin is too busy, I guess I'll hang out with my BFs!" Like I wasn't one of them! What's gotten into her?????!

Tuesday 4:30 pm

Aliesha's mood is even worse. She had a major sulk-a-thon yesterday when I got back from Ben's. And today at lunch she didn't appear until about five minutes before the bell rang for afternoon classes. I am sooo worried about her. We ALWAYS have lunch together. It's a Best Friends' Club thing. It's a twin thing. Why would she go off by herself?

Tuesday 8.45pm

Earlier this evening, Ben came over.

"I've been waiting for you in the park," he said angrily.

"But why?" I asked, petting his scruffy dog, Sam.

"Because we arranged to walk the dogs!" said Ben.

"No we didn't!" I cried.

"We arranged it today, Noelle!" he insisted. So we went over to the park and sat on the swings in silence. I almost apologized, but I stopped myself. What did I have to apologize for? I hadn't made the date in the first place.

Wednesday 5:30 pm

I've decided to keep a chart of all the missed dates with Ben, to help me figure out what's going on.

Okay, so, anyway, this morning I went over to meet Ben, so we could walk to school together, and he wasn't there. His mom told me that he'd already left. But wait, it gets weirder! When I asked Ben about it, he said that I told him that I was going to walk to school with Aliesha and the other BFC girls.

I SOOO didn't say that. How is our relationship going to work if this keeps happening?

Noelle and Ben's date chart

When?	Details of date	Explanation
Saturday	Ben said I'd canceled our DVD night.	No idea!
Tuesday	Ben told me I was late for dog-walking, but I don't remember making a date.	No idea!
Wednesday	Meeting Ben to walk to school, but he said I'd told him not to wait.	No idea!

Thursday 5:30 pm

I'm so worried about Aliesha. She seems so unhappy. What's wrong with her? And what's wrong with Ben? Everything feels different between us since all this unexplained stuff has been going on. I mean, we still talk loads—that's all okay. It's just, I get the feeling he thinks I'm disorganized and ditzy . . . which is totally NOT TRUE. It's just not fair.

Friday 6:34 pm

I spoke to Kaitlin today about all my mysterious date problems with Ben and she suggested talking about it at the BFC meeting. At first, I wasn't sure because I don't like it when everyone focuses on me, but Kaitlin managed to persuade me.

Saturday 2:14 pm

The BFC meeting was officially a disaster. I'm not joking. When I asked everyone's advice about Ben, Aliesha leaped to her feet and yelled, "THE WHOLE WORLD DOESN'T REVOLVE AROUND BEN MICHELSON, YOU KNOW!" and stomped out of the room.

Huh? Like, what's that supposed to mean?

Sunday 6:46 pm

I went over to the Brookbanks Dog and Puppy Rescue Center today, where I help out as a volunteer. Ben met me afterwards for a pizza, but I couldn't get what Aliesha said out of my mind. What did she mean?

Monday 6:24 pm

Major major developments!

Okay, so, I was walking past the lockers after gym,

when I spotted Aliesha talking to Ben. She was wearing MY pink t-shirt. She must have snuck it out of my room when I was out or something.

This is what they were saying:

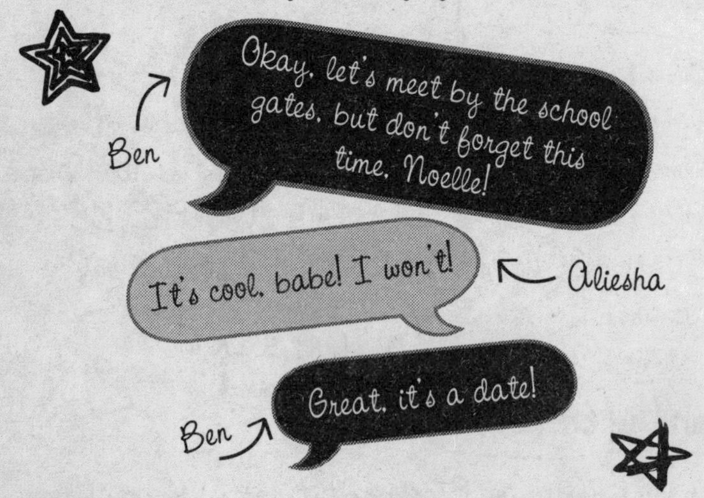

Yes!!!!!!!!! I am not joking!!!!!!!!!! Aliesha was pretending to be me!!!!!!!!! In my pink T-shirt!!!!!!!!!! Making a date with Ben!!!!!!!!!!

Suddenly, everything started clicking into place. Aliesha's moods. The messed-up dates. Everything. Aliesha had been deliberately trying to sabotage my relationship with Ben . . . but why? I burst into tears

and rushed past them. Two minutes later, I was huddled in the girls' bathroom with the rest of the BFC (minus Aliesha, obviously.). Nobody could believe what Aliesha had done. Especially me.

"I'm going to get Ben," said Addison, patting me on the back and slipping out of the door. After five minutes more crying, Ben and Addison appeared. I've seriously got no idea how she smuggled him into the girls' bathroom without anyone noticing.

"Where's my sister?" I sobbed.

"I don't know, hon," Ben replied. "She ran off when we saw you in the hall. She must have realized you'd figured out what was going on. No wonder we were getting confused with our dates. Aliesha was meddling!"

"But why did she do it? Why?" I cried.

"I'm sure Aliesha's got a weird Aliesha-ish reason," said Ben. Then, there was a sniff from one of the stalls.

"I have," said a shaky voice.

It was Aliesha! She appeared from one of the stalls.

"Noelle, I'm sorry," said Aliesha in a small voice. "I . . . I was so, so jealous. You were spending all your

time with Ben . . . and I thought you'd have more t-t-time for me if you two w-weren't together, so I . . . I tried to break you up."

"You should have just told me how you were feeling," I sobbed into Ben's sweater.

"I was hoping you'd just KNOW!"

"I'm not a mind-reader," I pointed out. "And I've never had a boyfriend before, so I never really thought about it." Doh! How could I have been so thoughtless?

Then Ben said the best thing possible. (He is totally awesome!) "I don't want to come between you and Noelle," he said to Aliesha. "She's been worrying about you for ages now. She knew you were unhappy."

"We've all been worried about you," nodded Addison.

"Nobody wants to see you unhappy, Aliesha," said Kaitlin.

"But, then again, nobody wants to see you dress up in Noelle's pink T-shirt and pretend to be her, either," said Calista wisely.

"I'm sorry, Noelle," Aliesha whispered.

"It's okay," I whispered back.

Aliesha sniffed, and smiled, and started to cry.

Tuesday 5:20 pm

Aleisha and Noelle's new twin rules

1. Never leave each other out.
2. Never pretend to be your twin without your twin's knowledge.
3. Always make time for each other.

"Oh, come here!" said Ben, putting one arm around Aliesha and one arm around me.

"Group hug!" yelled Kaitlin and suddenly we were all laughing and hugging each other and none of it mattered anymore.

Ben has been totally understanding and supportive about yesterday. He bought me a big box of chocolates to say sorry for doubting me over all the missed dates AND he invited Aliesha to the movies with us on Friday.

"I know you promised to spend more time with her, so let's all go together," he said.

"Then I can hang out with both of you!" I cried.

"Hey, why not invite the whole BFC gang, while you're at it!" Ben laughed. "It's not often I get to take out five gorgeous girls!"

"Okay!" I giggled.

"Cool! Let's all meet at your house at 6:30 pm," said Ben.

"It's a date!" I yelled happily.

My Diary
by Aliesha

Saturday 9 am

It's the weekend. Two whole days without school. What's not to love? But this morning, I felt totally, utterly miserable. I shut my eyes and snuggled under the comforter, hoping to go back to sleep. But it was useless. I knew exactly what was wrong. I was feeling guilty about Ben and Noelle. I knew Noelle, Ben, and even the BFC had forgiven me for pretending to be Noelle and trying to split her and Ben up. But I wasn't sure I'd forgiven myself. I was so used to having Noelle totally to myself that I couldn't bear the thought that she had someone else. Even if that someone else was as nice as her boyfriend Ben.

There's only one thing to do. I'm going to have to prove that I really am a good person, even if I forget to show it sometimes.

Ways to show I'm a good person.

1. Stop devouring celeb mags, like my fave mag "The Juice," from cover to cover and do good, selfless acts instead.
2. Stop daydreaming about celeb love god Mickey Dean and start doing good,

selfless acts instead.
3. Make some BFC meetings about raising money for charity.

Saturday 10 am

Here's how I put my plan into action:

Me:

Noelle, I could take care of Max today if you and Ben want to go to that theme park you've been talking about.

Noelle:

But I didn't think you liked Max.

Me:

(crossing my fingers behind my back): I LOVE Max. I'll take him for a nice long walk and (trying not to gag) I'll even scoop up his poop!

EEEWWW!!

Noelle was pretty surprised, but finally she agreed. She's left me a really long list of things to do for Max. To tell the truth, I don't like him that much. I mean, he's totally cute and everything, but his fur gets everywhere, especially all over my clothes. But this is about me showing Noelle that I really am sorry, so I will make sure I'm the best dog-sitter in history. Mom and Dad are out for the afternoon, so it's totally down to me. Hmm. . .

What to do for Max:

1. Max eats three bowls of dog food every day. He will eat any flavor except chicken. He hates chicken. If you put it down for him, he will pretend to eat it, then spit it out somewhere else.
2. He drinks two bowlfuls of water a day.
3. When taking him for a walk, always take him past the pond. He likes to watch the ducks.
4. He likes being scratched really hard behind the ears.
5. He likes to be picked up and sung to. His favorite song is "How Much Is That Doggie In the Window." He will bark along.

Honestly, anyone would think she was going for a year, not for a day. I mean, how hard can looking after one very small dog be?

Saturday 2 pm

This dog-sitting business is a total breeze. I've fed Max (and made sure it wasn't chicken-flavored dog food), given him water, scratched him behind the ears, and even sung to him. I couldn't quite bring myself to sing "How Much Is That Doggy in the Window," though. Instead I sang some of Beat Boyz greatest hits. Max's tail wagged so hard I thought it was going to fall off. I can't wait to tell Noelle that her dog has seriously good taste in music!

Ooh, hang on, I've got a text.

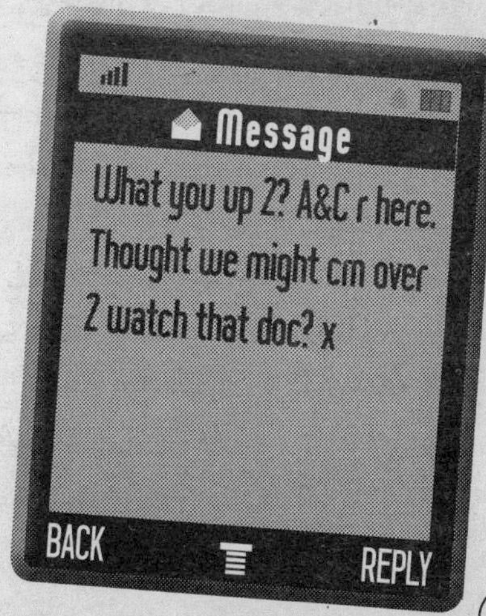

Awesome! I can tell the girls my idea about making some of the BFC meetings about raising money for charity. Max is curled up in his basket in the kitchen. I haven't taken him out for his walk yet, but I could do that after the documentary. Anyway, he looks totally comfy and cozy in his basket. It wouldn't be fair to disturb him. See, I really have turned over a new leaf. Being a good person actually isn't that hard.

Saturday 5 pm

OK, so I spoke too soon. Calista, Addison, and Kaitlin showed up at around two-thirty. Excitedly, I patted Max on the head, and left him still curled up as I went to answer the door.

"I can't believe you're dog-sitting!" said Calista, shaking her head in disbelief, as I got busy in the kitchen making grilled cheese sandwiches and milkshakes.

"Why not?" I said. "Max is pretty good company. And, you'll never guess what? He's a big fan of the Beat Boyz." I filled them in on our songfest.

"Speaking of which," said Addison, tapping her watch, "The Beat Boyz documentary starts in five minutes."

"So why are we standing around here?" I practically shouted. "Everyone grab a plate and move, move, MOVE!"

Fifteen minutes later we were all transfixed as the camera closed in on Mickey's piercing green eyes.

"Whatever!" said Calista, climbing off the beanbag where she was lounging.

"I need another milkshake. How about you guys?"

"Yes, please!" we chorused.

A couple of minutes later, she was back.

"Um, guys," she said worriedly.

"Shh!" I snapped. "The interviewer's just asking Mickey about his love life."

Calista picked up the remote and turned off the TV. "This is more important," she said.

I glared at her. What could be more important than Mickey Dean's love life?

"Aliesha, I don't know how to tell you this, but Max is missing, and the front door's open!" she said.

"But it can't be!" I jumped to my feet and ran into the kitchen, all thoughts of Mickey Dean wiped from my mind. Max's basket was empty. I ran into the hallway and stared in horror at the open door.

"But I closed it when you guys came in, I know I did!" I said, sinking onto the stairs. "Didn't I?"

Kaitlin sat down next to me.

"You couldn't have, Aliesha," she said gently. I buried my head in my hands. Why oh why didn't I take Max for a walk earlier? Then he might not have escaped out of the front door.

"Max is so tiny. If he's gone far, he'll never find his way back," I whispered. I knew I had to do something, and quickly.

"OK," I said. "We need an emergency meeting of the BFC. Now!"

Five minutes later we were all sitting in the kitchen.

"Right," I said, "this is what we'll do. Addison, cos you're Events Organizer I want you to figure out the different ways Max might have gone, so we can split up and search."

"On it," said Addison, jumping up and grabbing Dad's map from the shelf by the sink.

"Kaitlin, as Club Designer, I need you to make some posters we can put up. You can design them on my computer and print them out," I explained.

"I'll get started right away," said Kaitlin, heading for my bedroom.

"Calista, once we've got the routes figured out, you can help me and Addison look for Max," I said. "In the meantime, just keep your fingers crossed."

An hour later we'd searched everywhere we could think of. But there was no sign of Max.

"What are we going to do?" said Kaitlin.

"I don't know," said Addison. My phone vibrated in my pocket.

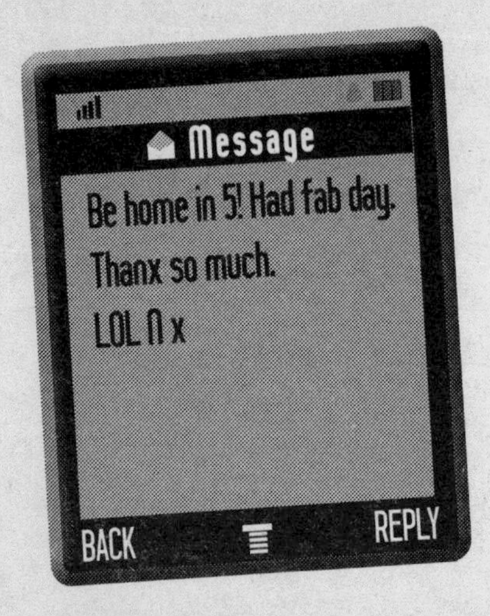

I looked at the others. "There's only one thing we can do," I said, trying not to cry.

"I'll just have to tell Noelle and hope she can forgive me."

Five minutes later, the front door slammed. Feeling sick, I shakily stood up. Calista gave me a smile of encouragement. Noelle stuck her head around the door.

"Hi guys!" she smiled happily.

"Um, Noelle . . ." I said.

"Oh Aliesha," Noelle grinned, "thanks so much for today. Look what Ben won for me!"

She bounded into the room, waving a toy dog. "It looks just like Max, doesn't it?"

"Noelle, I've got something to tell you," I said.

"Give me five minutes," she said. "Gotta go to the bathroom. Desperate!" Heading up the stairs, she looked over her shoulder. "Thanks again, Aliesha. You're the best sister ever!"

I followed Noelle up the stairs. I wasn't sure she'd ever forgive me for this. And to tell the truth, I wasn't sure I'd ever forgive myself either.

As Noelle came out of the bathroom, I cleared my throat.

"Um, Noelle, there's something I really have to tell you."

"What is it?" said Noelle, smiling at me as she headed into her bedroom.

"It's about Max," I said miserably. How in Mickey Dean's name was I going to tell her? How? How? It would break her heart.

"Don't worry," she said, beckoning me into her room. "I already know."

"You do?" I said, totally shocked. She must have seen the posters on the way home. I walked into her room, staring at the floor in shame.

"He's sleeping on your fave top," she said, gesturing at the bed. "I'm sorry. I borrowed it yesterday and forgot to put it back."

I stared at the bed in disbelief. Sure enough, there was Max, curled up asleep on my best top. I slapped my forehead. In our panic, we hadn't even thought about checking upstairs. I ran over and scooped up the astonished puppy, laughing as he licked my cheek.

MY DIARY BY ADDISON

Thursday 4:30 pm

Invite | Block | Send File | Save | Display Pictures

To: Aliesha4eva, SmileyNoelle, Calista100, Kaitlin.New.Girl

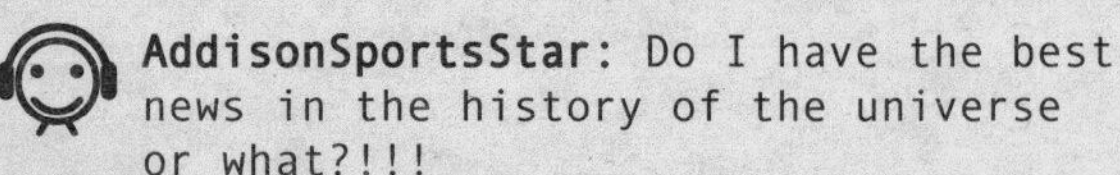

AddisonSportsStar: Do I have the best news in the history of the universe or what?!!!

Kaitlin.New.Girl: Spill, spill!

AddisonSportsStar: Ms. Street has just asked me to be captain of one of the girls' teams for school sports day!

SmileyNoelle: Hey Addy, that's fantastic. Good job!

AddisonSportsStar: Thanks! But there is some not-so-good news.

Calista100: Wotsup?

AddisonSportsStar: Ms. Street has gone and chosen Dopey Sophie—that's Sophie as in "Hey my best friend is Dina the Diva"—to be the other sports captain.

Kaitlin.New.Girl: Who cares? Our team is going to win anyway—no problem with you running it!

Send

Thursday 8:30 pm

I am supposed to be doing my homework but I can't concentrate. I am way too excited to worry about that when I have a winning team to pick. Ms. Street says I've got to decide who I'd like to be in my team but that I can't tell anyone before I tell her. This is like totally cruel! I mean, why should I have to keep secrets from the BFs? I mean, how can I keep secrets from the BFC? It goes totally against the rules. For starters, one of the BFC Club rules that we all agreed on, and I quote:

Promise 2 Never spill any secrets
Promise 5 Never leave any club members out
Promise 7 Treat each other with respect

BUT, I SUPPOSE IF I DON'T DISCUSS WHO I'D LIKE IN MY TEAM WITH ANYONE IN THE BFC, I WON'T BE KEEPING SECRETS WILL I?

Thursday 9 pm

I HAVE HAD A FEW THOUGHTS!

1. AS A SPORTS MANIAC I NATURALLY WANT MY TEAM TO WIN ON SPORTS DAY.
2. TO HAVE A TEAM THAT WINS ON SPORTS DAY I WILL NEED TO PICK ONLY THE BEST.
3. NATURALLY I WOULD LIKE TO HAVE ALL MY BFs IN MY TEAM.
4. NIGHTMARE THOUGHT: ALIESHA IS GOOD AT SPORTS. NOELLE AND CALISTA AREN'T BAD. BUT KAITLIN DOESN'T REALLY LIKE SPORTS.

Friday after school

I gave Ms. Street my team list today. So did Sophie. But Ms. Street said we'd both chosen quite a few of the same girls. Now we're going to have to take turns picking girls out at our next PE class (a TOTAL mega-nightmare).

Monday 8 pm

It's official. Kaitlin hates me. So do the other BFs. We had to choose our teams today. Sophie won the toss and she didn't dare choose anyone before she picked Dina. So I got Aliesha. Then Sophie chose one of Dina's doormats and I took my chance to grab Noelle next. But before I got to Calista, I realized that, if I wasn't careful, Sophie would snatch Gianna. So Gianna had to be my next choice. Then she nabbed Kaitlin. That was a relief! So I snapped up Calista and then chose the best of the rest from the other girls.

My BFs weren't happy at lunchtime.

"Oh thank you so much, Addison," Kaitlin wailed.

"Yes," said Calista. "It's mega-kind of you to pick Gianna before you thought of me and Kaitlin.

"I just don't understand it," Noelle added. "Why didn't you pick them as soon as you could? Now the BFC isn't together."

"Well how could we be?" I yelled back. "I'm in this to win it. It's not my fault if Kaitlin sucks at sports."

There was a collective gasp from my friends. They glared at me in horror. I could see Kaitlin's eyes getting all watery, and Noelle put her arm around her.

#1!

"But it's true!" I whispered.

Then Dina approached with a sneer on her face. She'd obviously heard at least some of our conversation.

"Oh dear," she smirked. "Looks like the L-L-L-Losers might just have fallen out."

Sophie put her hand on Kaitlin's shoulder.

"It's great to have you on the winning team," she said.

"Yes," said Mel, another one of Dina's dweebs. "I was thinking you and I could talk about the design for our uniform." And off Kaitlin went with them. She gave me this look over her shoulder as she left, like I'd just sold her baby brother on eBay. The rest of my BFs looked at me, shaking their heads in disbelief.

Well, get over it! Now I'm even more determined to win. The others just looked at me.

Monday 9 pm

I decided to email Calista because she of all the BFs was bound to understand.

http: //www.bfcink.com

mail Inbox (3) Junk (2) Drafts Sent Deleted Folders Calendar

From: AddisonSportsStar@bfc.com

To: Calista100@bfc.com

Subject: Sports Team

Verdana 10 B I U

Hey Calista. You understand, don't you? I mean Gianna is so much better than Kaitlin at sports. It has nothing to do with not liking Kaitlin. You know it doesn't. But we have to win the tournament. OK?

http: //www.bfcink.com

mail Inbox (3) Junk (2) Drafts Sent Deleted Folders Calendar

From: Calista100@bfc.com

To: AddisonSportsStar@bfc.com

Subject: Sports Team

Gill Sans 10 B I U

Actually no, I don't think it is OK. You know I like Gianna. But I'd still rather have Kaitlin on the team. Some things are more important than winning. Like your best friends. OK?

Tuesday after school

Gianna is the only person talking to me. At least she seemed pleased that she was on my team. Ms. Street suggested that we should use lunchtimes to train, so I've told everyone on my team to get together tomorrow for our first session.

Wednesday after school

Today has to be one of the worst of my life. So, we all got together to train on the athletic field. Everyone on Sophie's team was dressed in gym clothes, but with matching sashes. They'd obviously been made by Kaitlin, with red ribbons, and had all these beads and sequins sewn on them. Dina said, in her loudest and most irritating voice, "Kaitlin, these are just sensational. Lucky us to have you and Chloe on our team to make us look so uber-cool".

Kaitlin was totally playing up to her, shrugging and saying it was GREAT to help HER team, all the time looking at me like I ate kittens for breakfast or something. The girls on my team looked down at our boring gym clothes. The truth is, I hadn't even thought about uniforms. Trouble was, my team just seemed to be focusing their attention on how cool Sophie's team looked.

Thursday

Kaitlin is so NOT talking to me. I stood behind her in the lunch line today and she ignored me, even when I asked her to pass a bag of chips. It's so not like her. Is she really THAT hurt??!!! It's only a sports team!

Then Aliesha told me that she'd been speaking to Kaitlin. She'd told her that the sashes that she'd designed with Chloe were just the start of their team uniforms. They are actually going to make complete outfits: shorts, shirts, the whole works.

Is Kaitlin just trying to show me up?

"But looking good doesn't make you win a race," I pointed out to Aliesha.

"Yeah, but if you don't feel good, you aren't going to win, are you?" Aliesha replied.

I had no idea that clothes meant that much to all of them.

What am I going to do? I can't even ask the BFs because Noelle hasn't called a single meeting of the BFC since this sports thing all started.

FRIDAY

I sat by myself in the schoolyard today. I'd tried to get everyone together for training, but everyone on my team made up excuses about why they were busy. I'm sure they were fibbing. I suck as team captain.

Then Noelle came up. "Mind if I join you?"

"Only if you can manage to squeeze into my party," I tried to laugh. Then I could feel myself about to cry. I never cry!

"Looks like you need a friend," Noelle said, giving me a hug.

"Actually, I need all my friends. The BFC. But I've blown it, haven't I?" I sighed.

"A little," Noelle said. "Remember that part in the BFC rules about being loyal to your friends? Maybe if you were loyal to them, you'd get back even more from them."

I thought about what Noelle said all afternoon.

I couldn't concentrate in class. Then, when I got home, I figured that I had nothing else to lose.

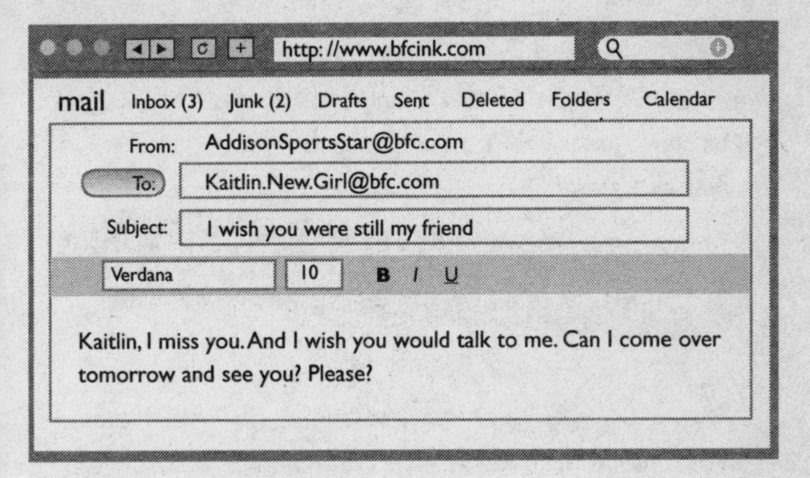

http://www.bfcink.com

mail Inbox (3) Junk (2) Drafts Sent Deleted Folders Calendar

From: AddisonSportsStar@bfc.com

To: Kaitlin.New.Girl@bfc.com

Subject: I wish you were still my friend

Verdana 10 B I U

Kaitlin, I miss you. And I wish you would talk to me. Can I come over tomorrow and see you? Please?

Friday—much later

Kaitlin hasn't replied. But I've decided I'm going over there anyway.

Saturday

OK, so seeing Kaitlin wasn't easy, but fortunately she's, like, the Best.

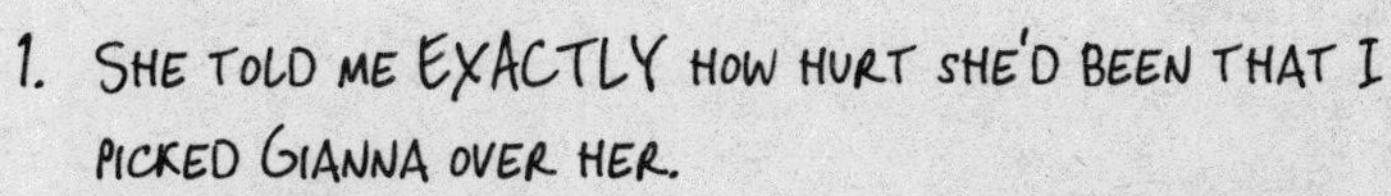

1. She told me EXACTLY how hurt she'd been that I picked Gianna over her.
2. She agreed she was a zero at sports BUT (and this was a completely fair point) she said:
3. she would have TRIED to win for me if I'd given her a chance.

I felt uber-guilty, but I still had to ask her if she was making cool uniforms for Dina's team just to make my team look lame.

And she said:

I just wanted you to see what you were missing.

SOB :(

Fair point. So I told her I was REALLY sorry and that I should have picked her over Gianna because Best Friends are more important than winning.

And she not only totally forgave me but she offered to help my team as well as Dina's. "After all," she said, "that's what BFs do!"

Like I said, Kaitlin is The Best.

Saturday morning

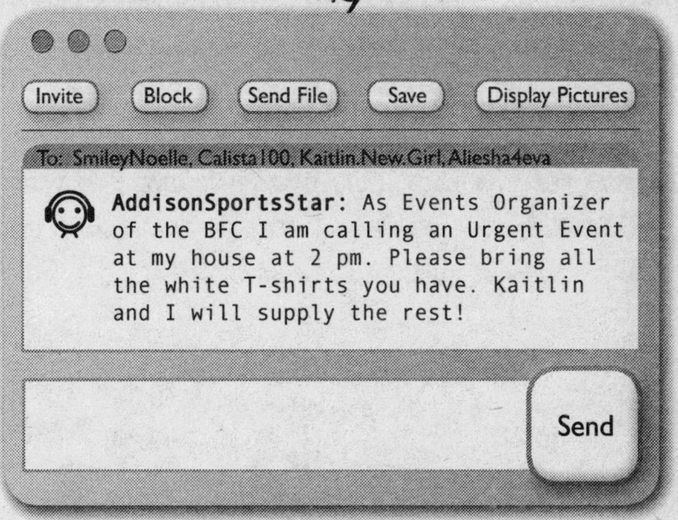

Late Sunday

I AM EXHAUSTED BUT FEEL GREAT! KAITLIN HAD THIS AMAZING IDEA OF DECORATING ALL THE T-SHIRTS FOR OUR TEAM. WE DECIDED TO CALL OURSELVES ADDISON'S JETS! WE USED ALL KAITLIN'S FABRIC PAINTS TO DO THEM AND THEY LOOK FANTASTICALLY AWESOME!

THEN THE BFs HELPED ME COME UP WITH A TRAINING PROGRAM. (WE USED KAITLIN'S KNOWLEDGE OF SOPHIE'S TEAM TRAINING TO MAKE OURS EVEN BETTER.)

NOELLE AND ALIESHA SAID THEY WOULD MAKE LOADS OF HEALTHY GRANOLA BARS TO GIVE TO MY TEAM AFTER EACH TRAINING SESSION. WE ALSO PLANNED A PARTY FOR AFTER SPORTS DAY AND MADE INVITATIONS TO GIVE THE TEAM.

ADDISON'S JETS ARE SOOoooooo GOING TO BE THE WINNING TEAM. IN FACT, (AND I CAN'T BELIEVE I'M SAYING THIS) EVEN IF WE LOSE WE WILL STILL BE THE WINNING TEAM BECAUSE WE ARE JUST GOING TO HAVE THE MOST FUN!

My Diary
by Calista
2-1=

Wednesday 6:15 pm

Yesterday, I was coming downstairs when I heard Mom and Dad talking in the hall.

"We can't afford it. Not with the way things are," Mom hissed.

"I know," Dad whispered back. "But it hasn't happened yet. Mackenzie's might still keep me."

My stomach did this weird kind of flipping thing. Mackenzie's is the company Dad works for. I walked downstairs extra loudly, so they'd know I was there, and they stopped talking. If you ask me, it's totally a sign that they're up to something. AGAIN! I'm suddenly feeling really worried. What if we have to move again, like when we had to go to Canada? I really, REALLY don't want to move.

Saturday 2:05 pm

Dad told us at breakfast that he's lost his job. He found out yesterday. He and Mom said I shouldn't worry and that he'll find another one soon, but I could tell from their faces, things were pretty bad.

"We'll just have to tighten our belts a bit," said Dad, in this totally fake-cheerful voice.

Saturday 7:30 pm

I've decided to find a way to help out. I mean, I can't get Dad another job, but maybe I can do something about the money. I am, after all, supposed to be a math genius.

Ok, so that was a total lie, but bowling and pizza are kind of expensive. Sure, I've got money left from my birthday—but if Mom and Dad are broke, we might need it for something really important. I'm just gonna try not to think about the BFC having fun without me.

Monday 3:55 pm

Dad might not have a new job yet, but I do! I know it sounds amazing, but it's true. Dad's been on the phone most of the day trying to find out about job openings. He had a long chat with a friend of his who works at the circulation department of our local newspaper, and it turns out they need someone to take on a paper route.

My dad thought I'd be really good at that but said he'd ask me first. So, as soon as I got home, he did.

"Mr. Alexander at the 'Daily Herald' needs someone to do a paper route, Scout," he said. "What do you think? Don't feel like you have to do it to help me and Mom out. I just thought you might like to earn a little extra spending money right now."

"Yeah, thanks Dad," I replied, thinking of all the things I could do with the BFC if I had more cash. "That sounds great."

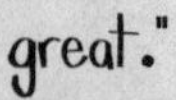

"Why don't you call Mr. Alexander back, so he can give you more details? His number's on the pad in the hall."

So I called Mr. Alexander and he asked me a bunch of questions. Then said the job was mine, as long as Mom and Dad agreed. I officially start tomorrow morning at 6:30 am—EEEK!

Tuesday 8:15 am

I haven't even had breakfast yet and I'm exhausted. Six-thirty in the morning is seriously early! I guess I'll get used to it after a few days. I'd cross my fingers, but it's hard enough riding my bike with a huge bag of newspapers over one shoulder as it is.

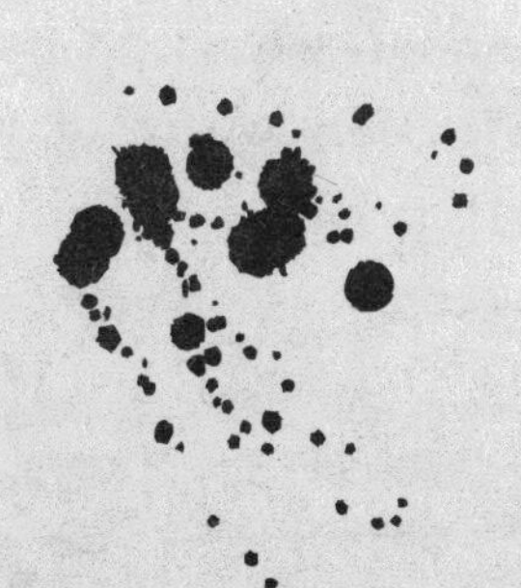

Friday 4:50 pm

The others spent half the day talking about their bowling trip tomorrow. I sooo wish I was going, but I had to keep pretending we're visiting Grandma. Addison's planning another BFC outing the week after next.

"There's this place you can go snowboarding indoors on fake snow," she said excitedly. "It'll be so cool."

"Totally freezing, in fact," grinned Aliesha.

I said I'd ask Mom and Dad if I can go, but there's no way I can right now. I'll just have to think up another excuse to get out of it.

I know it's no one's fault but I really hate missing out on the cool stuff the BFC does.

Monday: 6 pm

I'M SO TIRED! I have a massive pile of homework to finish, but my paper route is making me seriously sleepy. I almost nodded off in class this afternoon. I've also discovered a very annoying new scientific fact.

Doing a paper route every day + going to school + not having any fun = turning into a total grouch!

Wednesday 3:55 pm

Have I mentioned how totally and completely amazing my friends are lately? Well, they totally are.

At lunchtime, Noelle and Aliesha were talking about this new movie they want to see.

"It sounds really awesome," said Noelle.

"I read this review in 'The Juice,'" nodded Aliesha. "We sooo have to go this weekend."

They looked at me eagerly.

"I, uh, can't," I said. "I've got loads of homework."

"We don't have that much homework," said Aliesha.

"It wasn't the same going out without you last week," said Noelle.

"Just forget it," I snapped. "I can't go, ok?"

"What is wrong with you?" said Aliesha. "You've been in a bad mood for days. Anyone would think we'd asked you to join Dina's clique, not go to the movies."

"It's nothing," I shrugged, feeling guilty.

Noelle put her arm around my shoulders. "You can tell us," she said. "Best friends don't keep secrets, remember?"

And that was when I cracked. I was too tired and too miserable to keep it to myself anymore.

Noelle was right—keeping secrets from friends never makes anything better. I explained all about Dad losing his job, and trying to save money, then getting my paper route.

When I finished, Aliesha said: "I don't know about you two, but I sense an emergency meeting coming on."

Wednesday 8:15 pm

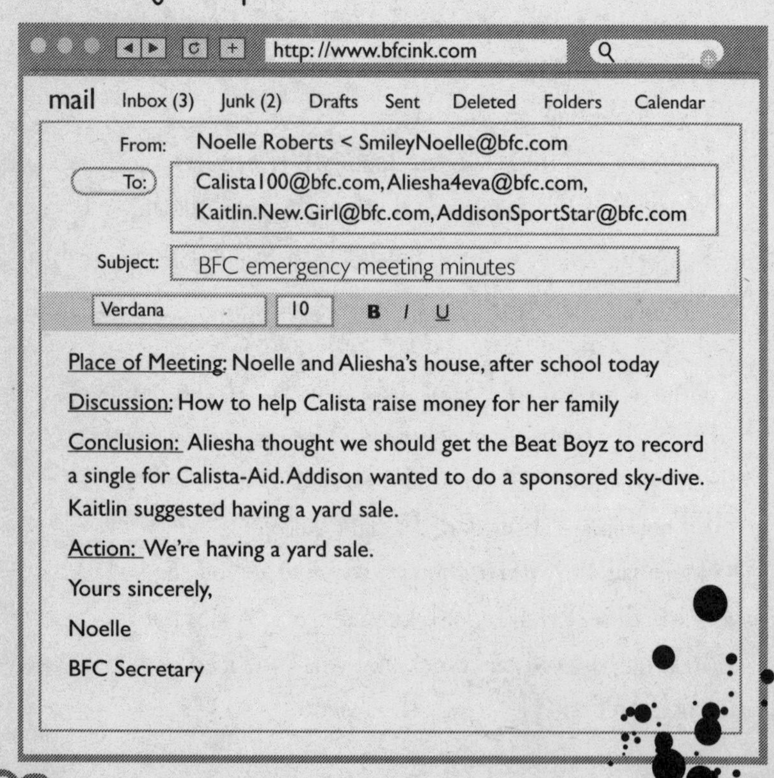

http://www.bfcink.com

mail Inbox (3) Junk (2) Drafts Sent Deleted Folders Calendar

From: Noelle Roberts < SmileyNoelle@bfc.com

To: Calista100@bfc.com, Aliesha4eva@bfc.com, Kaitlin.New.Girl@bfc.com, AddisonSportStar@bfc.com

Subject: BFC emergency meeting minutes

Verdana 10 B I U

Place of Meeting: Noelle and Aliesha's house, after school today

Discussion: How to help Calista raise money for her family

Conclusion: Aliesha thought we should get the Beat Boyz to record a single for Calista-Aid. Addison wanted to do a sponsored sky-dive. Kaitlin suggested having a yard sale.

Action: We're having a yard sale.

Yours sincerely,

Noelle

BFC Secretary

Friday 7:35 pm

So, yesterday, I asked Dad if he minded me taking stuff to a yard sale at Kaitlin's on Saturday.

"Of course, Scout," he said. (I hate it when he calls me Scout.) "Great idea. I'm busy on Saturday, though, so I won't be able to take you over there."

"What are you doing?" I asked.

"Is that the time?" he said, checking his watch, then he rushed out of the room. Seriously, just when I thought he'd stopped being so secretive.

Luckily, Kaitlin's big sister, Katie, has agreed to help us. We'll need all the help we can get. It's amazing how much stuff we've got—CDs, books, DVDs, computer games, some really ancient toys, clothes, and accessories.

Saturday 6:25 pm

If I was super-organized like Noelle and writing the minutes of today, I'd have to put:

Conclusion: Awesome!

Action: Celebrate!

Seriously, it was that good.

We all met at Kaitlin's again and Katie helped us unpack all of our stuff. Addison had brought this folding picnic table so we could spread everything out, and I'd remembered a box to put our money in.

We put the table at the front of Kaitlin's yard and started laying everything out.

"Hi," said a geeky-looking boy, who was waving from the house next door to Kaitlin's.

"Hi," I waved back.

"This was such a cool idea," said Noelle. "I bet we make lots of money." Half an hour later, though, things weren't looking quite so certain.

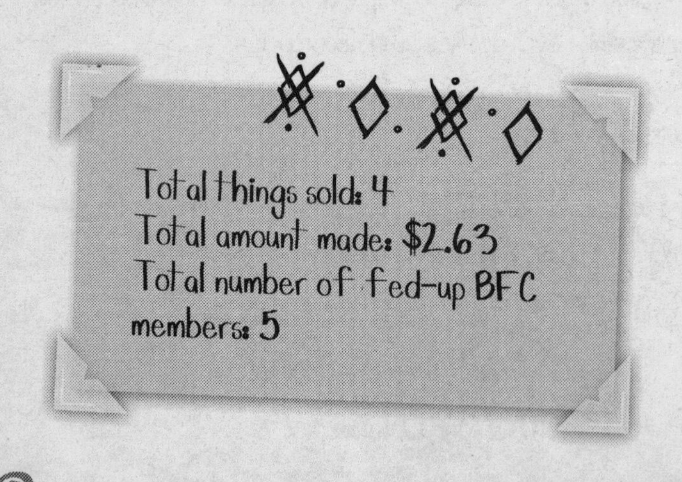
Total things sold: 4
Total amount made: $2.63
Total number of fed-up BFC members: 5

"Why isn't anyone buying our stuff?" whined Noelle.

"You're doing it all wrong," said a voice nearby. It was the geeky boy I'd seen when we arrived. Despite the geekiness, he was kind of cute.

"Excuse me?" said Aliesha.

"There are loads of people around. You just need to grab their attention. Make some signs, shout stuff out, let people know what you're selling."

We looked around, and realized he was right.

"Ok, guys, we need to do something," said Aliesha.

"Do we have any markers?" asked Kaitlin.

And before you could say "thanks, cute boy," we were bustling with new customers. Kaitlin had whipped up a couple of signs on the backs of old posters, saying things like "AMAZING BARGAINS" and "Best yard sale EVER."

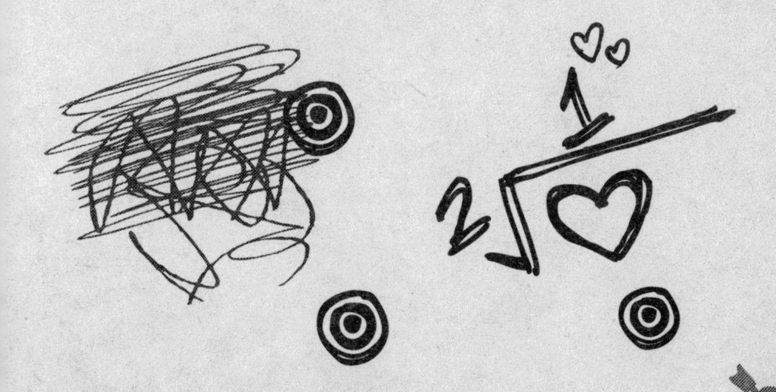

Aliesha was yelling her head off about all the cool things we were selling. Addison was rushing around, persuading people to come and look, and Noelle and I were busy serving customers, two at a time.

"That was insane," said Addison, when the sale was over.

As Addison and Noelle started to fold up the picnic table, my cell beeped.

"We should really say thanks to that boy," said Noelle, looking around to try and spot our friendly neighbor.

"It was mostly because of him."

"Did you see where he went?" Addison asked me.

"Who?" I asked, flipping my phone open.

"Geek-boy," said Aliesha.

"No," I said.

"You looove him," giggled Noelle.

"I do not," I said, blushing. I mean, he was kind of cute...

"So, how much money did we make, anyway?" asked Addison. I didn't answer. I was too busy reading the text on my cell screen.

"Hello? Earth to Calista," said Addison.

"Who's it from?" asked Noelle.

"Dad," I said, a grin spreading across my face. "He says the reason he couldn't help us this morning was because he had a job interview."

"And?" said Kaitlin, expectantly.

"He got the job!" I swear we couldn't have been happier if Dad had just landed a starring role in a Hollywood movie.

Aliesha squealed and all four of them jumped up and down, giving me an excited group hug.

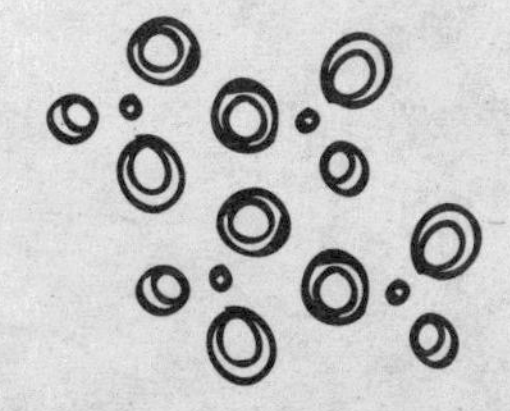

"There's just one problem," I said, when we'd calmed down a little bit.

"The job's not in Canada, is it?" said Noelle, looking worried.

I shook my head and grinned. "What are we going to do with all this money?"

"Let's see. There's pizza and bowling and snowboarding . . ." laughed Aliesha. "Believe me, we're gonna have a ball, BFC!"

My Diary
by Kaitlin

monday 7:30 pm

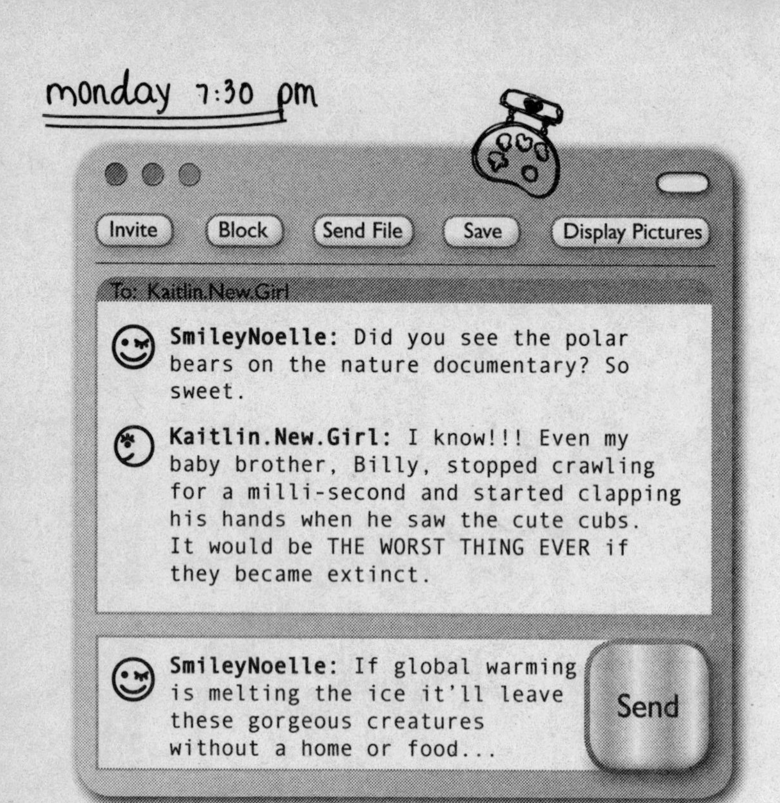

There must be something we can do to try and help . . . but what?

Okay, so Jen, (my stepmom and Billy's real mom) hasn't given up disposable diapers yet, but we recycle practically everything else. The trouble is, I'm not sure if everyone else does, and I can't change the world on my own . . . or can I?

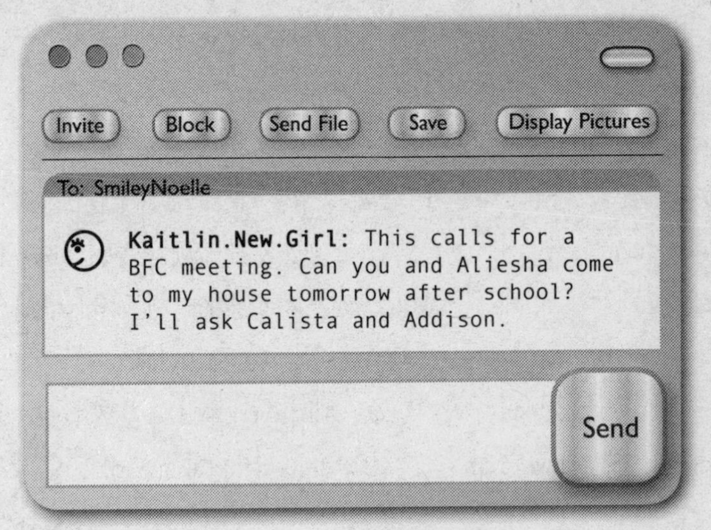

tuesday 7 pm

BFC to the rescue!!! We have just come up with the BEST plan ever.

"So what's the big emergency?" Aliesha asked, when I'd settled everyone down with drinks and snacks.

"Yeah," Addison nodded a little grumpily. "I'm missing basketball practice for this. It better be good."

"Plus we have a ton of homework to do," Calista grumbled. "Ms. Street is giving us more than ever."

Noelle looked at me. "Go on," she said.

"Um," I began nervously. Whenever I've mentioned environmental issues in the past, certain members of the group (mentioning-no-names-Aliesha-and-Addison) like to groan and fake-yawn. I was determined to get their full attention this time. "So, me and Noelle were watching a documentary all about polar bears last night," I continued.

"Ooh, me too," cried Aliesha. "It was so sad."

"I have to admit, even I was a little choked up," Addison added. "The image of those adorable little cubs on the melting ice . . ."

"I know. I had to switch channels, I was so upset," said Calista quietly. "If only we could go there and take care of them ourselves . . ."

"What we CAN do, though, is help raise awareness of the effects of global warming," I beamed at my fellow clubbers. "So, I was thinking . . . maybe we could do a 'Help the Planet' day to educate everyone in school about the benefits of recycling—just one way we can all do our bit for the environment. Dad says that the reason some people don't recycle is because they don't know enough about

it. We could put on some events and charge a little bit for kids to attend. All proceeds from the day could go towards making our school as environmentally friendly as possible. What do you think?"

"I love it!" Aliesha clapped her hands. "We could each do something to help raise the cash."

I practically had to kick everyone out of my house at the end of the meeting, we were all THAT excited about our "Help the Planet" day. We wouldn't just be helping polar bears by changing the way we live. Basically EVERYTHING would benefit from it, too. We're gonna check it out with Ms. Street tomorrow.

wednesday 4 pm

She bought it! Ms. Street totally LOVED our idea! Although not everyone shared her enthusiasm. Everyone meaning Dina Hart.

"Girls, this is fantastic," Ms. Street said, after we finished telling her our plan this morning.

"Let me have a quick word with the principal, Mr. Chester, then I'll make an announcement in assembly."

Which she did!

"Good morning, everyone," Ms. Street began, addressing the whole school in the auditorium. "We have some exciting news for you . . . next Friday Green Meadow will be involved in a 'Help the Planet' day. The idea originated with five pupils in my class: Kaitlin McCarthy, Addison Jackson, Aliesha and Noelle Roberts, and Calista Knight. I believe the idea came to them after watching a documentary about the effects of global warming on the natural habitat of polar bears. Kaitlin, would you like to tell everyone what you and your friends will be doing to try and help?"

Of course I wouldn't. WAS SHE CRAZY? I hate speaking in public. Noelle grabbed my right hand and squeezed it hard before I took a deep breath and (shakily) told the school what I'd told the BFC the night before.

Later, back in class, Dina had something to say.

"I don't get it. How will one 'Help the Planet' day help the polar bears?" she sniffed.

Mel, a friend of Dina's, came to my rescue. "Kaitlin's idea alone won't help the polar bears," she explained, "but just imagine if it took off. What if other schools did the same thing? It would help the environment—which means a better future for polar bears."

Good for Mel! I beamed at her in thanks.

"So how will other schools know what we're doing?" Dina asked. "It's such a waste of time."

"That's it!" I squealed in excitement. Another fabulous idea came to me. I almost felt like kissing Dina. Almost. Which reminds me...gotta go and make an important phone call.

wednesday 4:30 pm

There have been times when I've wanted to divorce my older sister, Katie. Not this time, though. Uh-uh! This time I felt like giving her a medal or something. Which, of course, I can't, since I'm not in charge of anything...yet!

Anyway, where was I . . . oh yeah, Katie. So, the conversation went like this.

I told Katie about my idea:

We're trying to raise awareness about the environment at school...

Katie replied:

Sounds good, but I can tell from your voice there's more...

I gave a nervous giggle and said:

I was wondering if you could run a report on our "Help the Planet" day in "The Juice."

Katie got excited. It was easier than I thought!

That sounds awesome. My editor wants me to do some "real life" pieces, and this could be perfect for the next issue!

I put the phone down and squealed. Everything was going according to plan. For once.

thursday 8 pm

http://www.bfcink.com

mail Inbox (3) Junk (2) Drafts Sent Deleted Folders Calendar

From: Noelle Roberts < SmileyNoelle@bfc.com

To: Kaitlin.New.Girl@bfc.com, AddisonSportsStar@bfc.com, Calista100@bfc.com, Aliesha4eva@bfc.com

Subject: BFC minutes (i.e. stuff we said and did)

Verdana 10 B I U

Place of Meeting: Thursday, Aliesha's and my house,

Discussion: "Help the Planet" day

Objective: To raise as much money as possible to green-ify Green Meadow, including (but not restricted to) the following:

- school to stock up on recycled paper
- change all light bulbs to energy-efficient ones
- place recycling bins in every classroom

Action: Kaitlin will make buttons with "green" slogans on them. Addison is going to manage the event (since she is the BFC's Events Organizer). Aliesha is going to make up a "Help the Planet" song and help Kaitlin make and sell stuff. Calista is going to hold a lunchtime cookie sale and, with every cookie sold, she'll give out a sheet that tells everyone what the ozone layer actually is. I'm going to tell everyone about global warming during my walk-your-dog-athon event. Katie is going to run a scoop for "The Juice" magazine.

Yours sincerely,

Noelle
BFC Secretary

I designed some cute buttons for everyone to wear.

And I made each member of the BFC their own "Help the Planet" name tags to wear:

friday 7:45 pm

I can't believe what has just happened!!!! I did some designs for "Help the Planet" buttons and stuff. And guess what? Jake just called me IN PERSON to ask if I could do a

"Help the Planet" skateboard design for him!

The rest of the day was a HUGE success too (I LOVED Aliesha's song), but we're all dead tired now. We must have raised a small fortune. Speaking of which, I wonder if anyone remembered to pick up the proceeds.

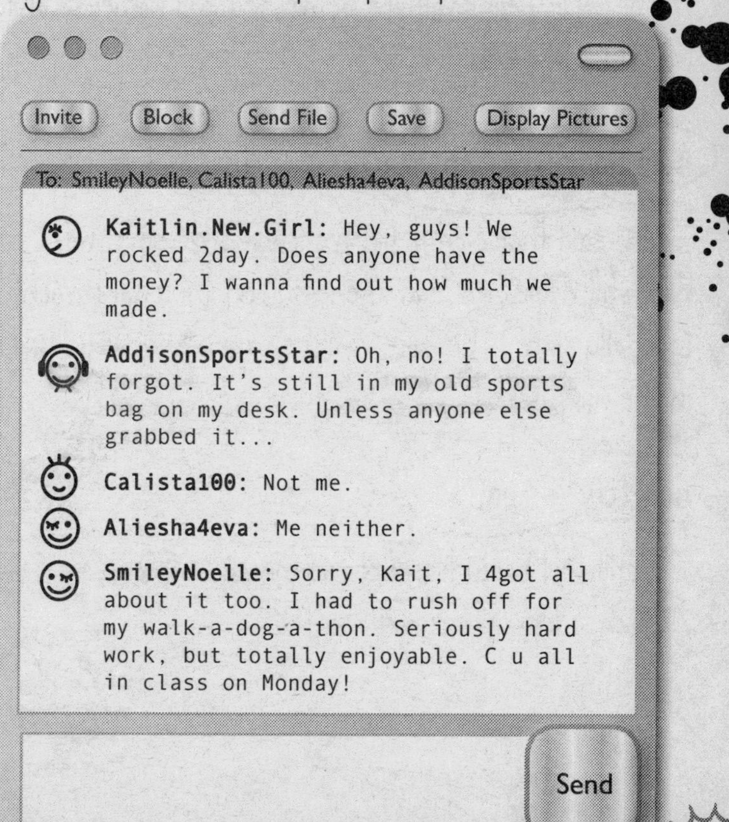

friday 8 pm

Oh, no! What if the money isn't there on Monday?

saturday 11 am

The polar bears will still be hungry and homeless and it will all be MY FAULT...

saturday 11:30 am

Jen said that even if the money was missing, we have still helped raise awareness about the environment. Especially since "The Juice" will be running an article on it in the next issue.

sunday 5 pm

I still feel bad. Please let the money be there on Addison's desk in the morning!!!

monday 4 pm

It wasn't there! I couldn't believe it! Well, actually I could. Of course it wasn't going to be there. THIS IS MY LIFE, AFTER ALL and nothing ever works out happily ever after. But, anyway, I was totally dreading seeing Ms. Street. What would she say when I told her that the money was missing?!

But when she walked in holding Addison's bag I breathed the biggest sigh of relief EVER. She'd taken it home for safekeeping. Pheew!

Katie's just texted me a pic of me and the BFC together. We SO ARE the Green Team!

BFC is The Green Team

Aliesha's **"Help the Planet"** song:

Help the Planet,
Join the team,
Together we'll build
Our green dream.

Around the globe,
No one will rest,
To help the polar bears,
They are the BEST!

Sort of like the BFC, heh, heh!

My diary
by Noelle

Tuesday lunchtime

I'm writing this while I'm waiting for Ben. He's half an hour late! I wonder what's happened to him? Maybe he hurt himself? Maybe he ate something bad in the school cafeteria or something? Maybe he's crippled with pain RIGHT NOW and is too weak to cry out for help or to text me and tell me where he is!!! Maybe he's . . . Oh, hang on, here he is . . .

Tuesday 4:56 pm

Okay, something strange is going on. A few weeks ago everything was going amazingly between me and Ben. All that stuff with Aliesha had blown over. Most nights we'd walk our dogs together, and on the weekends we'd just hang out and watch DVDs and stuff.

But then, two weeks ago, Ben started acting really, really un-Ben-like. First he stopped replying to my texts and then he started showing up late for dates or breaking them altogether. And then, well, basically, his entire personality completely changed. Seriously, it's like

aliens came and took over his body or something.

The weird thing is nobody else seems to have noticed.

And I'm just sooo bad at dealing with all this stuff. Like today, for example, I'd totally convinced myself that Ben was late because of some hideous cafeteria-related illness, so when I saw him, instead of saying, "Hey, why are you half an hour late?" I said, "Oh, Ben, you're all right!" and gave him a hug.

I can't figure out why he's acting so out of character and I know it sounds silly, but I'm too shy to ask. I mean, if he wanted to tell me, he would, right? And, anyway, I keep missing all the opportunities I have to ask—either Ben's best friend Jake comes along, or one of the BFC girls shows up, and well, I just never get the chance to ask Ben what's going on. I wish he'd tell me.

Tuesday 8:29 pm

Maybe I should ask the Best Friends' Club what they think?

Aliesha (who's my twin sister and chairperson of the club) thinks she knows loads about boy psychology, and Addison, our events organizer, has brothers, so she should know how a boy's mind works. And okay, so Kaitlin, our designer, says she doesn't know much about boys, but she's totally sensitive, and Calista, our club treasurer, always gives great advice . . . I don't know, though. I mean, I'd feel kind of shy about bringing it up at our meetings. I don't want to be the center of attention.

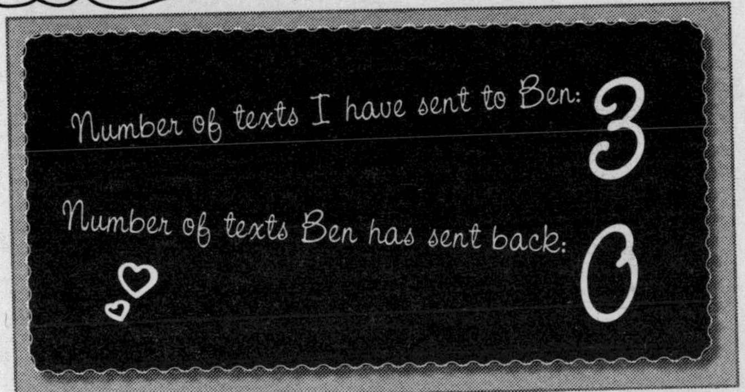

Mom just walked into my room and said, "Aren't you taking Max for a walk with Ben tonight?"

I didn't really know what to say, so I just kind of went: "Hmmm . . ."

"Is everything alright?" Mom asked softly.

I bit my lip and willed myself not to cry. Ben WAS supposed to be here at 4:15 pm, so where was he?

Mom stroked my hair for a second. I could feel my eyes welling up with tears. I kept them glued to my book until she shut the door, then I blinked and the tears started gushing down my face. Max jumped onto my lap and tried to wipe them away with his little nose.

Oh, why has Ben changed? Why? Why?

Thursday 7:30 pm

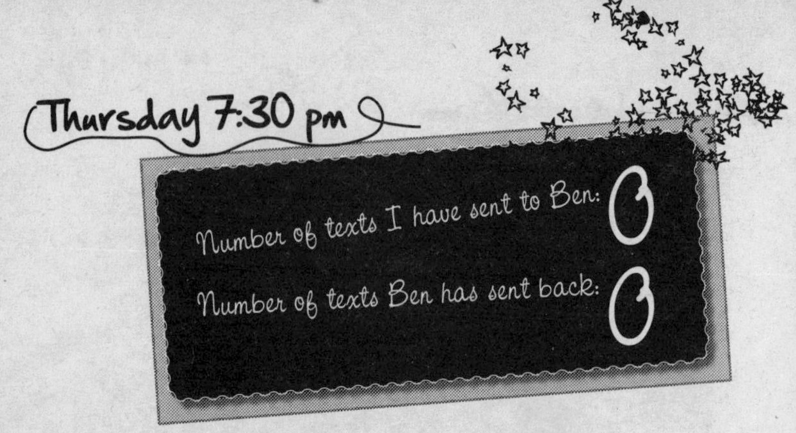

Saturday 4:33 pm

I went to the Brookbanks Dog and Puppy Rescue Center today. I used to volunteer every weekend but after I adopted Max, I became a pool volunteer, which means I don't go every weekend. I used to spend time with Ben, too, but it's been a while since we spent a whole Saturday together. He keeps saying that he's busy, like today, he told me he already had plans, but then I overheard him telling his best friend, Jake, that he wasn't doing anything. Maybe he doesn't want to go out anymore? I WISH I had the courage to ask him what's going on. I'm just so shy.

Going over to Kaitlin's later for a BFC meeting, but I don't really feel like it today. I just feel so down.

Saturday 4:43 pm

Just had a thought!!!!!!!!!!!!

Seriously!!!!!!!!!!!!

What if Aliesha is getting all funny again like before??? What if she is??? That could explain why Ben is acting strange!!! I mean, I hate to think that of Aliesha, because she promised me she'd talk to me if she was feeling left out. But what if she's pretending to be me again? What if she's trying to sabotage my relationship with Ben? She's done it before.

Oh, this is soo aaawwwful.

Saturday 5:20 pm

Uh, okay. So I asked Aliesha. I just came right out and asked her. Which, btw, is totally not like me, but I must be getting brave in the face of all this romantic trauma.

Then Aliesha said:

> I can't believe you'd think I'd do it again, Noelle. I learned my lesson. I know how much Ben means to you and I really like him . . . although he has been a bit strange recently.

Yes!!!!! Aliesha had noticed Ben's weird behavior, too!!!!! I stared at her for a minute, then suddenly I started talking. I talked so fast, my words practically tripped over each other. It all came out—the missed dates, the lack of texts, the lateness, EVERYTHING.

Aliesha listened and nodded, stopping me every now and then to ask questions. And when I finally finished, she said: "I think this is a problem for the BFC. Let's talk about it in tonight's meeting."

Okay, so Aliesha totally knows how much I hate everyone focusing on me during meetings, but I think she's right—I've got to stop being so shy and talk to the girls. Only the BFC can help me now . . .

Saturday 9:46 pm

It's weird. Telling the BFs about Ben really wasn't as hard as I thought it would be. Even when everyone's eyes were on me, it didn't feel like they were staring, it just felt like they were all listening . . . which was actually kind of nice. AND the best thing of all is that

we've come up with a plan!

"We need to do some detective work—find out if Ben has some kind of stress-related problem," Aliesha said. Kaitlin and Calista nodded.

"Maybe he's just being moody?" Addison said slowly. "It could be just a boy thing?"

"But this is more than that. I'm sure of it," I said.

"Well, Jake and Ben are best friends," said Addison, after a minute. "Maybe he'll know if Ben has a problem. I could do some snooping around if you want?"

"I think we've got ourselves a plan!" cried Aliesha. So now I just have to wait and see what Addison finds out.

Sunday 7:03 am

No news from Addison...

Sunday 7:15 am

Is it too early to call?
Better wait for half an hour.

Sunday 7:33 am

Maybe I'll just send Addison a little text. Yes! It's the perfect solution. I mean, if she's asleep, one tiny beep won't wake her up, will it? But if she's awake she'll answer back. See? Perfect!

Sunday 6:30 pm

Developments! Developments! Ben's family is moving! Addison overheard Jake and Ben talking about it. She just happened to be right outside Jake's bedroom door, you know, just checking the keyhole for dust, when she heard Ben tell Jake the whole story. Apparently Ben's mom got a new job with a top company in Rockington, so the whole family is moving.

But guess what? BEN DOESN'T WANT TO GO!

Does that mean that he doesn't want to leave me? And if so, why is he acting so weird? I mean, he's not acting like he's going to miss me very much—is he?

I'm going to talk to him right NOW. I have to!

Sunday 10:34 pm

What a night! Seriously!

Okay, so this is what happened after I knocked on Ben's door. . .

"Hi, Noelle," Ben said.

"I-know-about-you-moving-to-Rockington," I said all in one breath.

"Oh." Ben sighed, crouching on the doorstep to pet Max. Ben looked up at me for a second. "Do you mind if we walk the dogs? It's easier to talk walking."

Five minutes later we were in the park.

"I didn't want to tell you about moving away," Ben said, unclipping Sam's leash.

"But why?" I asked.

"Well, everything was so perfect. We were both so happy . . . and . . . I didn't want you to feel as sad as I do about breaking up."

Suddenly, everything became clear.

"Were you behaving badly on purpose?" I gasped. Ben nodded.

"So I would WANT to break up with you? So

I wouldn't feel as sad as you do, about you moving away?" I said.

"Yes," Ben whispered. "I'm so sorry, Noelle. I didn't know what else to do. I was just trying to protect your feelings. I thought if I could make you think I wasn't worth bothering with, then it wouldn't be so hard on you . . ."

I looked at him for a second then I gave him a hug.

"I don't want to break up, Noelle," Ben whispered.

"Me neither," I whispered back.

It felt like a huge weight had been lifted from my shoulders. Ben wanted to stay together! I hugged him as hard as I could and we held on to each other for ages. Then suddenly, Max and Sam started nudging our legs with their noses.

"I think they want to play 'fetch'!" grinned Ben.

I threw a ball and we watched the dogs race across the grass.

"You know," I said, "not that long ago, Calista's family moved to Canada. The BFC set up a webcam so we could talk to her. We could do the same thing. You know, when you move to Rockington."

"Great idea!" cried Ben. "We could webcam during the week and visit each other whenever we can on weekends! I could come down on the train and stay at Jake's! I could even bring Sam to visit Max!"

"That sounds perfect!" I said happily.

We sat on the grass and watched the stars come out and I knew in my heart that everything would be okay.

"How soon can you call a BFC meeting?" Ben asked. "Because if we're going to have a long-distance relationship, you guys will have to show me how to work that webcam!"

"There's a meeting tomorrow," I said.

"Perfect!" laughed Ben, as he put his arm around me and gave me a hug. I will miss him sooo much, but whenever I see him again it'll be even more amazing!

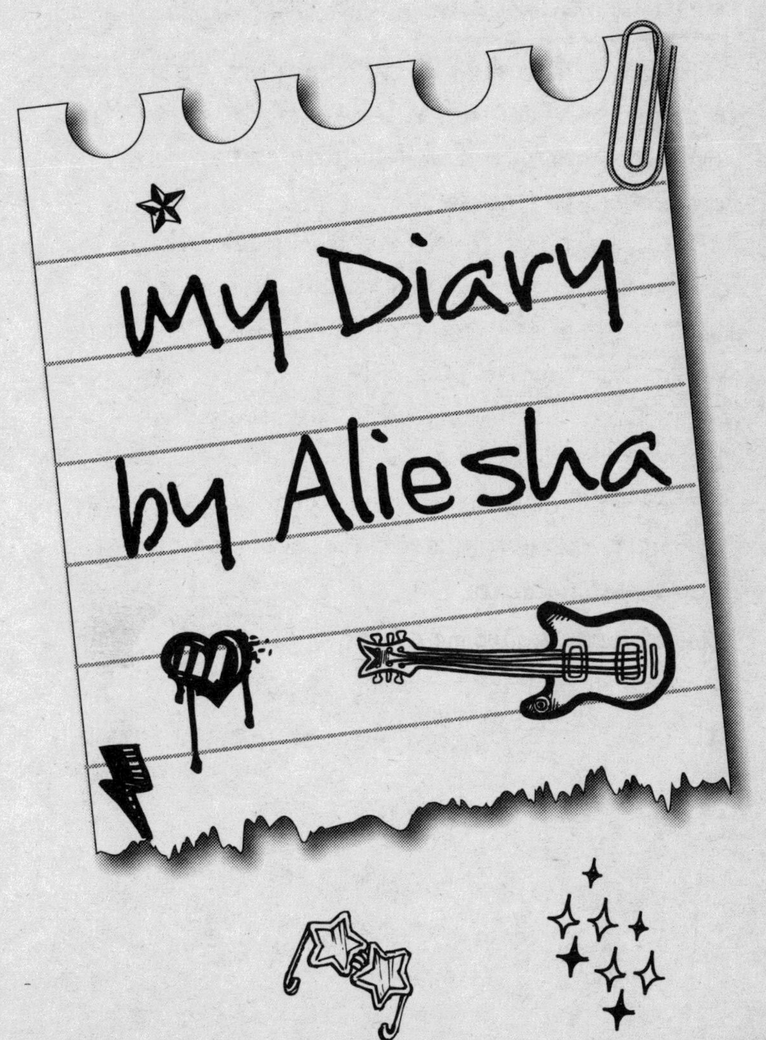
My Diary
by Aliesha

Tuesday 7:30 am

Today is the day when all my wishes are going to come true. Oh yes indeedy. World domination, here I come. OK, well maybe not quite world domination, but close.

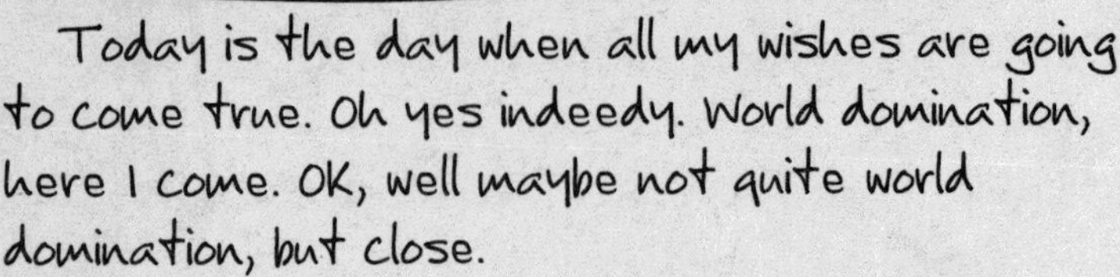

The auditions for the school production, "Grease," are being held today. And no doubt about it, the star part of Sandy has my name written all over it! The only thing standing in my way is Dina the Diva. But in my opinion there's about as much chance of her playing Sandy as me getting 100 in a math test: never going to happen.

I spent absolutely ages this morning trying to decide whether to:

a) wear my hair up à la good/if slightly boring Sandy at the beginning of "Grease."

OR:

b) use curling tongs to create Sandy when she goes glam and sings "You're The One That I Want."

But since Mom probably wouldn't let me out of the house with teased hair, and school has a strict no make-up policy, I decided that was a no-no.

Right. Time for a quick Sandy check before breakfast.

Tuesday 5:30 pm

My life is over. What happened, I hear you cry? Well, the auditions were a complete, utter disaster.

Dina the Diva was up first. She pranced around the stage dressed in a pair of PJs and some fluffy bunny slippers with her hair in pigtails. She looked more like she was heading for a sleepover than an audition. Obviously, she pouted, flicked her hair, and batted her eyelashes all the way through. And by the way she smiled smugly when she made her way back to her seat (making sure she accidentally-on-purpose stood on my foot on the way), she so thought she was going to get the part.

Then it was my turn. I was pretty nervous, but I'd practiced loads, so I hoped I'd be OK! It was deadly silent as I stood up on stage—you could have heard a pin drop. Nerve-racking or what?. I saw Noelle, who'd come for moral support. She crossed her eyes at me. Grinning, I took a breath and burst into song.

And, if I say so myself, I pretty much rocked it.

The whole room went crazy as I finished singing. Feeling good, I made my way back to my seat.

And that's when it all went wrong. Mr. Johnson held his hands up for silence, then walked toward where I was sitting with Noelle. I thought he was coming to congratulate me on my audition, but he didn't even look at me. Instead he crouched down on the floor in front of my twin.

"This is a little unorthodox, especially since you didn't sign up to audition," he said. "But I saw you sing in last year's talent show."

I stared at him, totally confused. During last year's talent show, I was performing a Beat Boyz track. Just as I went on stage I had an attack of nerves and almost ran off again. Fortunately Noelle stepped in at the last minute and we sang the song as a duet. Together we blew everyone away and won first prize. But what did that have to do with this? Unfortunately, I was about to find out. Mr. Johnson was still talking.

"Well, I just think that you'd be perfect as Sandy. You've got the perfect characteristics. So I'd like you to audition."

Me and Noelle stared at him open-mouthed.

"But what about Aliesha?" said Noelle.

Exactly. What about me? Anyone could see I was born to play that part.

Mr. Johnson cleared his throat. "Well, Aliesha's audition was very good. But I'd really like you to give it a go."

I bit my lip, feeling a sob building in my throat. This wasn't supposed to happen. Noelle was supposed to be here to support me, not steal the role from me! I looked at Noelle, who was staring at me.

"I won't do it unless it's okay with Aliesha," she said.

I opened my mouth to say no, actually it wasn't okay with me. But then I remembered I was supposed to be turning over a new leaf. And after everything I'd put Noelle and Ben through, I still had a lot of making up to do. So, fighting back my tears, I smiled at Noelle.

"No problem," I said. "May the best twin win."

I'm just hoping that the best twin is me!

Thursday 12 am

I'm sitting in the girls' bathroom writing this. The cast list went up today.

Grease

CAST LIST

Sandy : Noelle Roberts
Rizzo : Aliesha Roberts
Frenchie: Olivia Sanchez
Jan: Grace Aarons
Marty: Bella Hopkins
Danny: William Price
Vince: James Gordon

I took one look and headed straight for the bathroom, trying not to cry.

I DON'T BELIEVE THIS! I REALLY DON'T BELIEVE IT! I'M SUPPOSED TO BE THE STAR OF THE FAMILY, NOT NOELLE! THIS IS TOTALLY UNFAIR.

Ok, I should be totally happy for Noelle. After all I am trying to be a better person after I almost broke her and Ben up.

But it's like ALL the good things happen to Noelle. First she WINS the talent contest, then she starts dating Ben, and now she's been given MY part—even though she didn't even want it. Not like I did!

My one comfort is that at least Dina won't be able to gloat because she only got some teeny background role. Ha!

OK, better stop hiding in the bathroom and go and face the world.

Thursday 4 pm

When I opened the bathroom door, Noelle was standing outside, concern all over her face.

"Are you OK, Aliesha?" she asked. "If you're not all right with me playing Sandy, I'll go and see Mr. Johnson right now and tell him I don't want the part."

How is she so NICE all the time? There was no way I could ask her to give up the part (though there was a little bit of me that REALLY

REALLY wanted her to). But showbiz is showbiz. I owe it to my Art and myself to make the best of a bad deal. So I said, "I can't think of anyone I'd rather lose a part to."

And then I flashed her my biggest grin. "And you'd better watch out, cos I'm going to steal the limelight. I'm going to be the best Rizzo *Grease* has ever seen!"

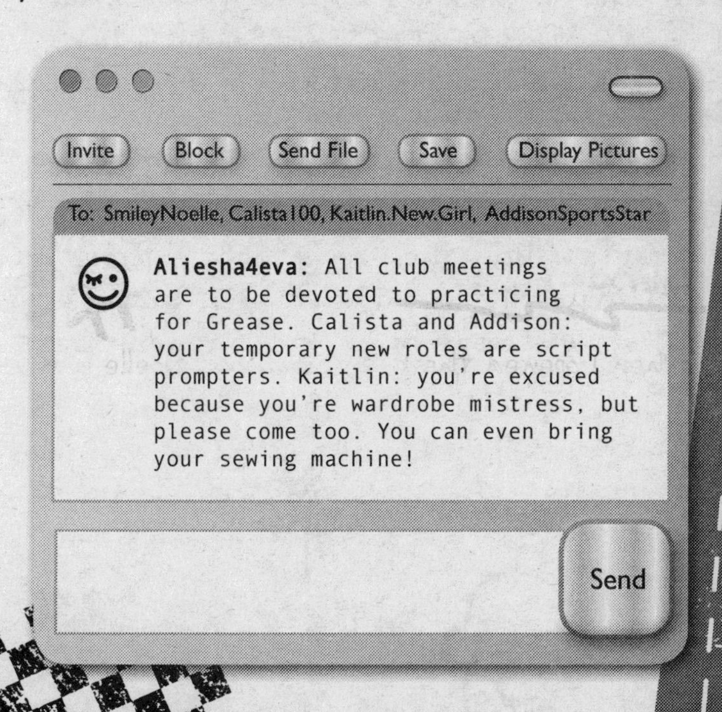

Thursday 6 pm

Can't believe the play is tomorrow! Boy, has it been hard work, but totally worth it.

And guess what? I'm loving the part of Rizzo! She's totally cool—a tough girl with a soft heart. A little like me, actually. And she has one of the best songs in the whole play. And you know what? I think Noelle is PERFECT for Sandy. All her goodness and niceness just kind of shines through. If I was Danny I'd totally fall for her too.

Plus, the BFs have been awesome AS USUAL. I'm not sure me and Noelle would ever have learned the parts without them being there to prompt us every step of the way. They've even arranged a BFC after-show party for us on Saturday. Best friends totally rock.

8 pm

Noelle's just gone to bed with a seriously sore throat. I so hope she's OK for tomorrow.

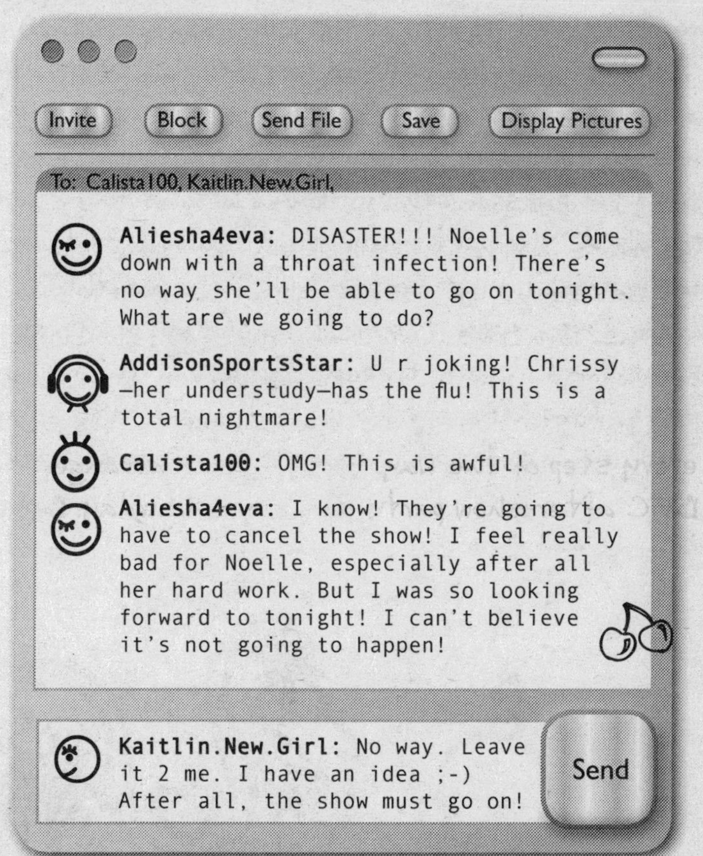

Saturday 10 am

I don't believe it. Mr. Johnson's just called. He wants me to play Sandy, since I know the part by heart and I'll fit into all her clothes perfectly!

Actually, I'm kind of sad not playing Rizzo. (me? fickle? NO WAY!) But the show must go on and guess what? Addison is going to play Rizzo– she's rehearsed with me so much that she could totally do the part in her sleep! Apparently it was Kaitlin's idea. I was so shocked, I dropped the phone. Possibly for the first time in my life I was totally and utterly speechless! I can't think of a better Rizzo (except for me, of course!) I've said it before and I'll say it again: Best Friends Rock!

After midnight (!!!!)

It was such an amazing night. The play was fan-triple-tastic! I actually LOVED being Sandy. At the end, Kaitlin came rushing on stage with a humongous bouquet of flowers. Seriously, they were almost as big as me!

"These are from the BFC," she whispered. "Just don't forget us when you're rich and famous!"

"As if!" I whispered back, obviously meaning as if I would ever forget them, not that I'm never going to be rich and famous. I was born to be rich and famous! That goes without saying ;-)

I couldn't stop grinning, especially since the audience wouldn't stop clapping until I agreed to sing again.

You see? I was BORN to be the star of the show. Yay!

When we got home, Mom had even made my favorite pizza with GOOD JOB ALIESHA spelled out in olives! And even Noelle managed to stay out of bed long enough to have a slice. I felt bad for her, but she said (well, she croaked) that it was okay and she was proud of me for saving the show.

I honestly don't think I'm going to sleep a wink, I'm on such a high. I can't wait till tomorrow to celebrate properly with the fabulous BFC!

MY DIARY BY ADDISON

Friday (late)

So here's my **GOOD NEWS**:

1. Go Greased Lightning! Aliesha SOoooooo rocks. She rocks so much even I've been dancing to the music from the school show. I mean, it was so sad about Noelle being ill. But all the BFs were so pleased for Aliesha.
2. That cutie (and Ben's friend) Elliot has been over to the house again!

And my **BAD NEWS** is:

1. Noelle's been sick (but she is getting better, requiring lots of BFC TLC).
2. My big bro Jake is mega-missing his best friend Ben since he moved away (which is sad for him but good for me because it means he spends more time with Elliot!)

Saturday afternoon

I do NOT understand boys. OK, so I spent all morning at the skate park giving it my all. If I say so myself, I did some good moves and some pretty amazing tricks. Anyway, Elliot was there with Jake today. He's totally smooth on that skateboard, I can tell you. But when I went over and tried to talk to him, to tell him how cool I thought his boarding was, he just kind of grunted at me and kept talking to Jake. I mean, like he couldn't care less what I thought about his skating. And there I was imagining that he sort of liked me. He's been smiling at me and talking with me when he's been over here. But today it was like he didn't even want to know me.

Like I say;: I do NOT understand boys.

SUNDAY 7pm BFC PARTY DAY!!! YEAAAAH!

We were all over at Aliesha and Noelle's house earlier for a meeting of the BFC. Well, it wasn't really a meeting so much as a party, to celebrate Aliesha's success and to make Noelle feel better. Noelle is just amazing. I mean, if I had been too sick to enter a swimming race or play in a basketball game, and someone else had stepped in for me and won or scored, I'm not so sure that I'd have been as pleased for them as Noelle was for Aliesha.

"Aliesha you were the best," Noelle croaked as we clinked our glasses of juice together to toast Aliesha.

"And you are the best twin sister a girl could ever have," Aliesha replied, hugging Noelle.

Calista had made some seriously cool chocolate chip cupcakes. Yummy-scrummy!

"And these are the best cupcakes a girl could ever have!" I said.

Kaitlin, being ultra-amazing at art, had made the most awesome banners for Aliesha and Noelle. The one for Noelle had loads of flowers and glitter and stuff on it and was really cute. Aliesha's said "Aliesha

ROCKS!" They were totally fantastic.

It was a great afternoon and, just before we were all about to leave, Noelle's laptop made a "ping" noise that told us all she had a message.

"Well, we know it's not from one of us," Calista said.

"So it must be from the gorgeous Ben!" Aliesha grinned.

Noelle's cheeks turned pink and I could tell that she wanted to rush over and read what it said. But she kind of held back, like she was embarrassed to look at it when her friends were still around.

I felt sorry for Noelle. Well, I think we all did. But I kind of felt extra sorry for Noelle because I think I know how much she likes Ben. There was a time when I thought he was cute too, but Noelle was much more right for him.

And now that Ben's moved away—HOURS away, in fact—I think it's extra cool that Noelle still hears from him. It must, as Kaitlin keeps saying, be TRUE LUHVE!

Anyway, we all told Noelle to go and chat with Ben.

Go, Noelle, Go!

Monday after school

It is SO sweet. Noelle told us all at breaktime today that she and Ben had chatted online for ages. I knew that they had because Jake was in a foul mood. He was trying to play a quiz game online with Ben all night (the kind where you answer all kinds of questions about TV shows, and geography, and people, and stuff). But Jake couldn't get Ben to respond, even though he "nudged" him about a million times. When I told Jake that I thought Ben might be talking to Noelle, he just rolled his eyes and grunted, saying "What's he interested in a girl for?"

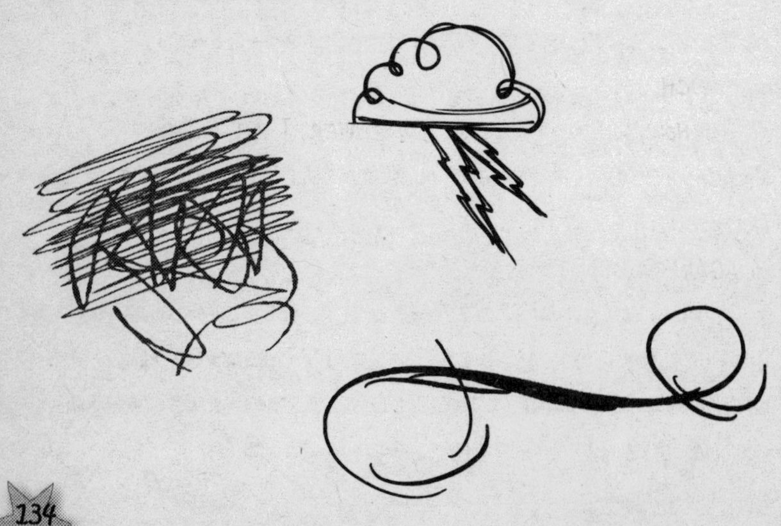

Tuesday after basketball

OK. So I was at basketball practice and we were playing at the recreation center. Jake was there playing pickup soccer with his friends, and Elliot was one of them. I saw them when they got there and I said "Hi" to Elliot. He said "Hi" back and seemed pretty friendly. He even said "See you later," which he did because, after doing some warm-ups, we played a game to practice some of the new maneuvers we'd learned, and Jake and Elliot came in to watch the end of the game.

I thought I was impressive because I got two baskets. Our coach, Ms. Knox, said I did a good job and that's praise indeed from her because she doesn't ever say much.

Anyhow, when the session was over, I put on my tracksuit pants and went over to the boys. Jake had promised to walk me home, you see. Plus, I wanted to say hi again to Elliot.

"Whoa, you stink!" Jake said in a really charming big brother sort of way. I could feel my cheeks burning with embarrassment. I knew I'd sweated during training, but did I really stink that much?

It got worse. Elliot started to giggle along with Jake. They were BOTH laughing at me. Terrific.

I told Calista all about it. Then she must have told Noelle because the next thing, I got an IM from her.

Hmmm. That was easy for her to say. She's got a boyfriend. Well, kind of.

Wednesday after school

I THOUGHT ABOUT ELLIOT QUITE A BIT LAST NIGHT.

WHAT I DO NOT GET ABOUT ELLIOT

1. ELLIOT SEEMED TO LIKE ME BEFORE. WHAT'S GOING ON?
2. MY FRIENDS ALL SEEM TO HAVE BOYFRIENDS, OR AT LEAST SOMETIMES GET BOYS INTERESTED IN THEM. I'M A LITTLE DIFFERENT FROM THEM BECAUSE I'M KIND OF SPORTY, AND DON'T WEAR GIRLY CLOTHES, ETC.
3. MAYBE IF I DID THINGS DIFFERENTLY, ELLIOT WOULD LIKE ME.

Wednesday 8 pm

I've been reading back issues of "The Juice" magazine all evening. Kaitlin gave them to me ages ago because her sister Katie works for the magazine. I flicked through them but they aren't really my sort of thing. I mean the stuff about the Beat Boyz was OK.

I'd rather read Skate magazines. But I figure that if I go through Juice I might pick up on some of the stuff the other BFs are into. Then I could get uber-cool and make Elliot notice me again.

Gotta go. I've got five more copies to read before school tomorrow and my Mom will go APE if she sees my light still on after 9 pm.

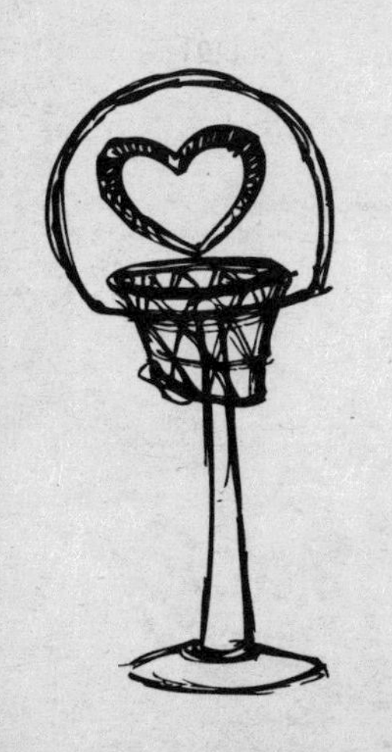

Thursday after school

1. I DID MY HAIR IN COOL PIGTAILS THIS MORNING.
2. I WENT TO SCHOOL. IF THE GIRLY LOOK WASN'T ME, THEN MAYBE A MORE FUNKY-PUNKY STYLE WAS.
3. I FOUND SOME OLD LIP GLOSS THAT ALIESHA LENT ME AGES AGO.
4. I WORE SOME FOOTLESS TIGHTS.
5. THE BFs STARED AT ME WHEN I GOT TO SCHOOL.
6. CALISTA ASKED ME IF I WAS OK.
7. I SAID OF COURSE I WAS OK AND WHAT DID SHE MEAN?
8. SHE SAID "UH, WELL, I GUESS YOU DON'T LOOK LIKE YOU USUALLY DO."
9. I SAID COULDN'T I WEAR WHAT I WANT, WHEN I WANT? JUST LIKE THEY ALL DID. I NEVER SAY ANYTHING ABOUT WHAT THEY WEAR.
10. THEN I WALKED AWAY.

Thursday 4:30 pm

I HATE today. Just when I thought things couldn't get any worse, they just did! I saw Elliot with Jake when they got back from school. He'd come over to do some homework with Big Brother.

"Whoooa!" Elliot said, flicking my pigtails. "What are these?"

Boys! I heard them laughing as I ran upstairs.

Thursday 6 pm

The BFs have just left. They are the best. They said they knew I hadn't invited them but they could tell that what I needed was some BFC TLC.

"So what's up?" Calista asked me. "Why are you so concerned with hair elastics all of a sudden? And am I right in thinking it has something to do with Elliot?"

I looked at her. How did she know?

"Addison," she went on, "if you are upset or confused about something, I want to help. Right?"

"Yes," I said, feeling pathetic. "But why is everyone else so worried about me wearing hair elastics? I do sports, don't I? It's not like I've never worn hair elastics before!"

"Sure," Calista said. "But not with wacky pigtails. What's it all about?"

"Well, maybe I felt like a change," I said. Which was sort of true. "But it obviously isn't worth it." And it's hard work, I thought.

"Why would you want to look like everyone else?" Calista asked. "What's wrong with being Addison?"

"Everything," I said.

"Addison, of course you are worth it," Calista said. "But I wish you would tell me what all this is about."

So I did. I told Calista all about how I thought Elliot didn't like me and that maybe if I changed the way I looked, Elliot might start noticing me again—in a good way. I'd tried the girly look and that made me feel stupid and look stupid. The sporty look didn't work either. But then this look made everyone laugh at me! Why couldn't I get it right like everyone else?

The BFC all listened and I cried a little. They gave me a group hug. "We all think you are great just the way you've always been," Aliesha said. "Think about it. You are:

1. Great at sports.
2. Really popular at school.
3. One of the Best Friends anyone could ever have.
4. You wouldn't be a BFC if you weren't fabulous!"

"So you don't think I need to change?" I said.

"Of course not!" she grinned. "And if Elliot can't see just how amazing you are, it's his problem."

Hmmm. I thought about it. Maybe Elliot wasn't so great. And anyway it's hard work trying to be something you're not. And you know what? My best friends think I'm cool, and that's good enough for me.